Chimera

The Shippy Writers

ISBN 978-1-914381-40-9

The Shippy Writers

Chimera

For Colin.

Our official NON-FICTION section member

He's ALWAYS there ...

Tales

THICKER THAN WATER

James Lefebure

1.

The Heir Is Born

SUSAN FOCUSED ON her breathing. She ignored her dark hair, slick with sweat, sticking to her forehead. She tuned out her husband's words of encouragement. Useless as they were. He would never know the agony her body was experiencing. The pain gripped her once more. She let out a scream and pushed.

'Please be a girl' she whispered to herself as her body tried to expel the baby.

She could feel her body straining. Muscles contracted and pushed. Something was coming. Her breathing was controlled as she exhaled. Pushed. Another breath. Another contraction. Another push. Thus, it continued.

'I can see the head,' her mother informed her. 'It's nearly over, Susan.'

Her mother's cool hand was on her head. They exchanged a look. This was the moment. Another child brought into their family. The weight of expectation nearly crushed the breath out of her drained body. *Please. Be a daughter,* her mind begged any god that might have been listening.

Another wave of contractions. Breathing rapidly, she let out a final scream. It filled the cabin. Her hopes and dreams washed through the pain. The moment was upon them. Her mother reached down as Susan felt something pass through her. Tears sprang to her eyes. A sharp crying filled the house. Her mother worked fast. She had delivered all the children in this family. Susan knew her child *(Daughter. Please. Be a daughter,* her mind babbled) was in capable hands.

'Is it?' she managed to whisper.

She didn't want to know the answer. She needed to know the answer. Everything was riding on what was in between the legs of the child she had just brought into the world.

With a tenderness she expected, her husband, Neil, cut the cord linking her to the baby. He clipped something on as her mother pulled him aside.

Neil and Barbra stood at the end of the bed, cleaning the babe. Thick silence suffocated the room. Tears filled Neil's eyes. He smiled for a second. This was followed by a deep realisation of his future. Reading the face that she'd known since she was a child herself, she knew.

~~~~

'You have a son,' Barbra said quietly.

A wail of pain escaped Susan's throat. The silence shattered.

'No!' she screamed. 'No. No. No. No.' Susan's hysteria was joined by the crying of her son.

There was too much noise. It threatened to shatter her. Her world had changed. At that moment, she saw Neil holding their son to his chest. He had never looked prouder. In all their life together, she had never seen such a look of happiness on his face. She hated him at that moment. He had done this. She hated the child. She hated them both. How could he be happy in this moment? He knew what this meant for them. She could feel the tears creeping down her face. Barbra looked at her daughter crying.

'Shhh,' she soothed, her own maternal instincts kicking in. She tenderly wiped away the tears that cut a path down her daughter's face.

'My sweet girl. This is a happy moment.' She took Susan's head to her thin chest and stroked her damp hair. 'You should be proud,' she soothed as sobs wracked her own child. 'He is the first boy in the family in over eighty years.' She looked over at her son-in-law. They all knew what was next. 'Your father will be so proud of you, Susan,' Barbra whispered as she kissed Susan on the forehead. 'I am so proud of you.'

'Mum. Please. No.' Susan sobbed. The path they all walked down began now. In this moment. Susan wasn't prepared to travel it. Not now. Not ever.

'Take your child,' Barbra ordered.

The time for pleasantries had passed. Instead, tradition dictated the course of action. It was how they had been raised. It was what their family did. Without hesitation, Neil did as commanded and passed the child to his wife. There was nothing to say. Susan could have smashed the child's head. Bitten her husband. Screamed and burned the world to the ground. Instead, she took her son. She had been raised better than to fight tradition. She knew. In her broken heart, she knew. This was just the start.

'Your father would have been proud, Neil.' Barbra put a hand on his shoulder and squeezed. 'Look after her.'

He nodded. Tears welled in his brown eyes as Barbra turned away from him.

Her skeletal hand touched the baby's head.

~~~~

'Susan, you must look at me,' she ordered.

Years of obedience from her daughter compelled her to do as instructed. She hated herself for it. A smile spread across Barbra's face. To her daughter, she had never seen her mother look so serene. So beautiful and strong.

As her mother pulled the blade against her throat in a single motion, the smile only grew. Susan sobbed as the blood sprayed across her. Its warmth soaked through her top. It coated her face and the baby who was trying to nurse at her chest. With a heavy thump, Barbra fell to the floor. It had been done.

Susan looked at her son. He was unfazed by the wetness that coated him. She knew in that instant that despite the pain in her heart, she would love this child. It was what must be done. It was what she had been raised to do. If her mum was willing to make the sacrifice, then she could do the same. The blood stung her eyes, but she lifted her head and looked at Neil.

'I think we'll call him Liam. After your dad.' A smile spread across her face as she hugged her child.

'I'd like that,' Neil replied. He moved forward and picked up Barbra's ankles. 'I'll take her down. Give you some alone time.' His thin body strained as he pulled the body across the wooden floor.

'Neil?' Susan whispered.

He stopped and looked at his wife. 'Yeah?'

'I love you.' She smiled. 'I love our family.'

A smile spread across his face. 'I'll be quick. Then you can jump in for a shower.'

Holding the baby to her chest and rocking, Susan hummed. A son. It hadn't been what she wanted, but now that she held him, it felt right. The path was set. She would give herself to him. There would be pain; she knew that. Sacrifices would be made. She was a mum now. That's what motherhood was all about. As she wiped her mother's blood off her face, she looked at the bundle in her arms.

'I'm going to tell you all about your granny, my boy ...'

2.

Gan Gan Pays a Visit

THREE HEAVY KNOCKS on the door were all it took for Liam's four-year-old brain to light up like a firework.

'Gan Gan is here!' he shouted as he shot towards the door.

'Okay, sweetheart.' Susan chuckled as she got up from the couch.

'GAN GAN!' Liam shouted again, hopping from foot to foot.

Susan's heart lurched in her chest watching her son. In the last four years, her father had become a beacon of hope for her family. That was all going to change after tonight.

'Muuuum,' Liam whined as he tugged on her dress.

Looking at him, she couldn't deny the love she felt. It was her job to provide him with the tools he needed to be the best member of her family. She pushed her thoughts of the future away. She would focus on today. On her son's birthday. With an effort, Sarah pushed away the thought of his birthday gift from her father.

Opening the door, Susan genuinely smiled. All the worry in her mind melted away as her father stepped into the house and pulled her into a hug. She could smell his pipe smoke and the whisky he drank. The scent of her childhood. His beard tickled the top of her head. The hug was almost painfully tight, but she didn't mind. Looking down, she laughed as she pulled away from him. Liam was hugging her father's leg. His deep laugh joined her own as he bent over and picked up his grandson.

'Looks like someone is happy to see me.' David's laugh faded out as he looked across the living room. With a simple nod of his head, the mood changed. 'Neil.'

Susan felt the tension increase as her husband came across and shook her father's hand. There was less time than she imagined. Was that always going to be the case?

'Hi, David, was all he said before putting his hand round Susan's waist. 'Everything's sorted, he whispered to her.

Susan didn't want to hear any more.

'Liam, why don't you go and show Gan Gan the picture you've been drawing.' This was all the encouragement he needed.

'Come on,' Liam begged, his small hand leading his grandfather towards the middle of the room.

David laughed again as he allowed himself to be led away. A fleeting look passed between the three adults. Her father's laugh sounded hollower than it did a few minutes ago.

~~~~

Anger filled Susan's heart as she turned to her husband. 'Would it kill you to be nice to him today?' she seethed.

'I didn't say anything?' Neil responded, confusion written all over his face.

'Exactly.' She started to walk away from Neil. 'I can't believe you sometimes,' she whispered.

'This is hard on both of us, Sue,' he whispered back. 'I don't want to do this, you know. It's not something I'm looking forward to.'

Susan's anger started to dry up. Neil was right, of course. She knew that he didn't want to be part of this. They had both been raised for this eventuality but never thought it would be their child. She guessed it was the price they paid for the miracle that was currently showing his grandfather his artwork.

'Sorry, she conceded. 'It's just, today is harder than I thought.' She thought back to her mum. The only memory that she could muster now was the smile on her face as she cut her own throat. It had eclipsed all other memories. Neil pulled her thin frame into his arms and held her for a moment.

She wanted to resist, to rage and scream. Instead, she buried her head into his chest and felt his heart beating. 'Let's just get through tonight as best we can.' This was bigger than them. This was tradition. It was family.

With a final squeeze, they parted. Susan went over to her son and father. Neil went back to the basement.

'Looks like we have a budding artist on our hands,' David offered when Susan sat on the couch.

'He's got an eye for it.' She smiled sadly. 'Just like you.' David did the same. A thousand unspoken words danced between them. 'He wants to be just like his Gan Gan, don't you, Liam?'

'Yes!' Liam smiled, bouncing on his feet. He was getting bored of showing his pictures now. Gan Gan felt sad, and he didn't like it. Everyone should be happy today. He was happy. Looking up at his mum and Gan Gan, he felt his tummy hurt. Nobody seemed to be smiling. They were pretending. His bottom lip started to tremble. He didn't want to cry. He was a big boy now. That's what his daddy kept telling him. Big boys don't cry. He didn't want anyone to be sad.

'This is for you,' he said, pushing a picture to his Gan Gan. It was a picture of them both.

David looked at the picture. It needed no explanation.

'Thank you, Liam,' he said and pulled the child in for a hug. 'Gan Gan is so proud of you,' he said as he rocked the crying child.

Susan couldn't watch any more. She wanted to fight tradition. She didn't want anyone to experience any pain. Instead, she went to the kitchen to get everything prepared. She could hear her father's deep voice talking to her son. Her instinct was to rush to him and see if she could sort what was ailing him. She ignored this. She needed to focus on her own pain first. She got the drinks ready. Approaching the fridge, Susan scanned the pictures that had been put on there. Liam had drawn all three of them together. The house was in the background. It was the type of art only a mother would love.

It would have been how her father had started. His oil paintings were pure art. He had a reputation that befitted his talent and had called for a hefty price tag. It was a skill that he would be passing to his grandson. It was tradition. With a heavy heart, she opened the fridge and took out the jug of juice. She set out her father's glass and poured. Neil would be back up soon. She got him a beer ready. He would need one before the night was done.

Returning to the living room, she saw that Liam had reverted to his normal energetic self. Her father sat smiling, watching his grandson. He looked up and saw that he was being watched. A sadness filled his eyes as he saw the glass. With a groan and clicking knees, David stood up. Susan walked up for another hug from him.

'Is it time?' David asked.

'Nearly. Neil is sorting out … the last bits.'

'He's a good man, Susan.' This meant everything to her. Finally, her marriage had the approval she had so desperately craved. 'He's been working out?' David noted.

'Yeah. He wants his gift to be something personal.'

'That is a lovely idea. He has a few years yet, but I think his dad would have been proud of that choice.'

'Me too,' Susan replied.

A click behind them both broke the moment. Neil had returned to the living room. The time was nearly upon them.

'Liam, honey, come here,' Susan called to her son.

She passed the glass to her father and the can of beer to Neil, who mouthed his thanks. His hands were trembling when he accepted the drink. She quickly returned to the kitchen and came back with a cup of water for Liam and a drink for herself. Returning to the living room, the three most important men in her life were gathered. It was a picture that she would try and hold in her mind. This wouldn't be like her mother. She wouldn't have to witness this.

Taking the lead, her father cleared his throat.

'I'd like to wish my grandson a happy fourth birthday.' He paused for a second, licking his dry lips. 'You are going to be a fine man one day. Like your father.' He looked at Neil and nodded his unspoken approval.

Susan could feel the tears threaten to fall. She bit her lip to stop them.

'I want you to remember, in the years to come, that your Gan Gan loves you very much.'

Liam picked up on the mood of the room as children are apt to do.

'Don't go!' he wailed as he wrapped his small arms around David's leg.

'I will never be far from you.' David hugged his grandson one last time.

Once free of the hug from Liam, Susan wrapped her own arms around her father. This was never going to be easy. There were many more goodbyes to say before the time came for her own. She needed to steel herself against this in the future.

'I love you,' she told him for the final time.

'You're doing us all proud, Susan,' he replied.

The void in her arms as he left their hug would never be filled. She knew that. Her family were everything to her and Liam. The weight of legacy rivalled that of Atlas. She didn't want David and Neil go to the basement. When the door clicked shut, however, she held Liam tight to her and they both cried.

3.

Sister, Sister.

THE ROOM WAS filled with laughter. Liam proudly wore the badge with a holographic 10 on it as he spoke to Corrina. He kept giving her increasingly strange multiplications to do and looked in awe at her as he put them in the calculator she had given him. She was right every time. Her sister, Annie, kept looking over at them both and smiling.

'He's grown so tall.' she exclaimed as if she hadn't seen her nephew every month for years. Family was important. It was tradition. It was taught from birth. Nothing comes before family.

'He's shooting up, isn't he.' Susan beamed back. 'He's taking after his dad now and working out every day,' she added with a smile.

'I can't believe how big Neil has gotten the last few years.' Annie blushed. It was no secret that Neil's previously thin frame had increased in bulk and strength over the years. He had a son now and wanted to be the strongest man in his life. Both figuratively and literally.

'Costs me a fortune in chicken and eggs.' Susan laughed.

'Okay. Okay. My brain needs a break now!' Corrina's laugh joined the chorus.

'One more,' Liam begged to no avail. When he realised that his aunt wasn't about to do another, he sulked over to the couch and flopped down.

'He's going to be a handful when he turns thirteen,' Annie commented. The comment hung in the air for a moment. They all knew what would happen when Liam turned thirteen.

Susan felt her stomach knot. It was three years today that it would have to happen.

'I'm so sorry, Aunt Susan,' Annie whispered. 'I wasn't thinking.'

Susan waved her hand, clearing the tension in the air. She knew that there was no malice in what was just said.

'Despite being a writer, my dear sister never seems to think about the words that come out of her mouth,' Corrina added with a thin smile. The three women started to laugh lightly. It was a hollow sound. 'Mum is always banging her head against the wall whenever Annie speaks,' she added.

'Oh, she was like that when we were younger,' Susan added with a genuine smile. 'She had no patience whatsoever. It used to drive Mum …' A memory of her mother's face as she slit her throat burst into Susan's mind. She coughed, and the twins exchanged a look.

'Thank you for coming tonight.' Susan changed the subject quickly. 'I can't believe it's come round so quickly.'

'It's family,' Corrina whispered. Her hand reached for her sister.

'We are more than happy to give our gifts,' Annie replied, putting her hand in Corrina's. 'And we're together.' Both women smiled.

Liam's birth had solidified a family belief. Since her father's birthday gift, Susan had learned to steel her heart on this day. She had been raised this way and would see her family wishes through to the bitter end. There would be hard times ahead; she knew that. She would pass through them. For her son. For her family. For her bloodline.

Looking over the living room, she saw Liam playing with the calculator. It was the first gift he'd ever received on a birthday. His face when he opened it had been a picture. Outside of Christmas, he never received presents. Everything was being kept for him until his 18th. Only then would he understand the love his family held for him.

'Evening, ladies.' Neil's deep voice interrupted her train of thought. She hadn't heard him come up from the basement. With his rapidly expanding frame, this was no mean feat. He had put on muscles she didn't know existed since her father's birthday present.

'It's time.' He addressed Corrina and Annie.

'Are you sure?' Annie asked. 'Could we not wait a little longer?' There was a fear in her voice that wasn't previously there.

'ANNIE!' Corrina hissed. 'Don't you dare bring shame to our mother.' Tears sprang to Annie's eyes. 'You were raised better.'

There was nothing else to say. Susan no longer did goodbyes. Instead, she simply looked at her nieces.

'Thank you for your gifts. I will ensure they are put to good use. For the family.'

'For the family,' the women replied automatically.

Liam didn't even look up as his aunts walked past with his father. He never asked where they were when Neil came out of the basement alone and went straight to the shower. He was asleep when Neil emerged from the bathroom.

4.

Daddy's Boy.

'LIAM,' SUSAN SHOUTED once again. She rolled her eyes and took a deep breath. "Count to ten," she whispered to herself. She got to three before she shouted again. "Hurry. Up." She could hear the mum voice and hated herself a little for it. After today, she would work on this. On her patience. She would have to.

'What?' came the grumpy reply as Liam walked out the bathroom.

'You were in there forever,' she scolded. 'I'm not spending your thirteenth birthday with you hiding in the bathroom.' There it was again. The tone. She took another deep breath.

'Where's Dad?' Liam grunted at her.

It had been like this all week. Neil and Liam had been together every day. She had tried to not allow herself to get jealous. It hadn't worked. Instead, she had nagged. She had cried. She had begged. None of it had come to much of anything. The sun still rose and set every day. Neil had continued to take Liam out of the house for the day and return without telling her what had happened. Looking at her watch, she knew he would be back soon.

'He's out,' she huffed and walked to the kitchen.

'I'm hungry,' Liam moaned.

In that exact moment, Susan hated her son. The entitled, spoiled, selfish young man she had created. The reason for her loss. Her fists clenched, and her heartrate sped up.

'You'll just have to wait,' she responded through gritted teeth. 'Go set the table.'

'Why?'

'Because I said so.' Susan could feel her fingernails cutting into her palm. The sharp pain helped to focus her rattling mind.

'Dad never has to set the table,' Liam provoked.

She decided to choose peace.

'You know where the cutlery is. Set the table.' She strode through the kitchen door straight into the bathroom. Instead of slamming the door and screaming, she gently clicked it closed.

Susan ignored the smell of shit that Liam had left in the air. She let the toilet lid fall down to allow her to ignore the stains on the inside of the toilet. The wetness on the edge of the bathtub soaked into her dress as she sat down. This was ignored as well.

Instead, Susan cried. A silent cry of a pain so deep there was no sound that could encompass the agony it was conveying. Through the bathroom door, the noise of the front door closing let her know that time was short. The bathroom was filled with Liam and Neil's voices in conversation. The words weren't clear, but oh, how they sounded alike. Liam's laugh cut through the house. The urge to go and scream at him was so intense she nearly sprinted out the bathroom.

To avoid leaving the safety of the small, tiled room, she picked up his towel. She poured bleach down the toilet. She re-arranged the shampoo bottles. She remembered how much she loved Neil. How she would always love the time they did have together. She splashed her face with cold water and counted to ten. Then twenty. The woman that opened the bathroom door was going to celebrate her son's thirteenth birthday. With her husband. She would cherish the next few hours. They were going to be her last with Neil.

She knew that after today, there would only be pain. She was a mother first. A wife second. She was doing this for family. For their future. Like with her mother, her father, and her nieces, the pain would pass. Her heart would harden. Liam would carry the family legacy forward. It was how she had been raised.

5.

Tongue Tied

'NUMELE MEU ESTE Liam și vreau să mănânc brânză,' Laura proudly replied.

Liam laughed in his dad's laugh. Susan's heart lurched.

'And what does that mean?' Liam asked.

'My name is Liam, and I want to eat cheese.'

Laura and Liam both burst out laughing. Even Susan joined in. Liam's love of cheese was a running joke for everyone who knew him.

'That's so cool.' Liam looked at his aunt in awe. 'I can't believe you speak Romanian, French, Japanese, and all those other languages.'

'I've been learning them since you were born,' she replied. A look passed between the sisters.

'How's Julie?' Susan asked.

'She's good. Same as Liam, really. Sixteen and ready to take on the world. Aren't they all at that age?'

'She'll have to come round for tea again. You had a nice time with her last week didn't you, Liam?' Susan smiled a little as he blushed.

'Yeah,' was all he could say. Both women smiled. 'She's so cool.'

'Awww,' the sisters said in unison before laughing.

'Shut up,' Liam said, his beetroot face unmissable.

'Why don't you go do the dishes for your mum,' Laura instructed her nephew. 'There's a good lad.'

Liam did as he had been requested. The last three years had changed his attitude. He was growing into a man that she could be proud of. Now, it was just the two of them.

'Sounds like Liam and Julie are getting on well?' Laura enquired

'Oh, they were laughing and joking something fierce,'" Susan confided. 'And they shut the bedroom door.' Susan waved her hand. 'I just left them to it.'

'Mum used to do the same with you and Neil. Remember?' Laura smiled sweetly.

Sarah did remember. Stolen kisses, whispered declarations of love, and plans for a family. The plans they used to make in her small bedroom. Looking at her life now, she knew she had achieved everything they had planned.

~~~~

'I still miss him,' Susan confessed.

'I don't think that will go away.' Laura was the more practical of the two.

'I'll miss you.' Sarah felt the lid of her emotions start to slip. 'It's just going to be me after today.'

'Liam is worth it.' Laura's matter-of-fact tone firmly put the lid back in place. 'I've not spent sixteen years learning all the languages I can for nothing, you know.' A smile touched her thin lips. 'You'll need to look after Julie, though. She'll miss me.'

'I promise I will. I just pray that they have a girl when the time comes.' Susan's confession would be sacrilegious to anyone but her sister. 'It's so much harder than Mum and Dad made me believe it would be.'

Laura nodded as she reached forward and took her sister's hand.

'You'll have to make sure they marry next year, Laura whispered, 'and … hold off on the wedding night until …'

The two women sat in silence, the weight of family expectation crushing the words they both wished to speak. At that moment, they were mothers. Sisters. Wives. They were frightened about the future. Holding hands, just like they did as children, they didn't need to share a word.

'You want a brew?' a voice shouted from the kitchen.

The moment was shattered. The time had come. There was to be no more delay to the inevitable.

'I'm all right, thanks, love,' Laura shouted back. 'I'm going in a minute.'

Liam walked into the room. 'Already?' he asked glumly.

Susan envied his ignorance. It wouldn't be there for much longer.

''Fraid so. Come give your old auntie a hug.'

Liam did as he was instructed without hesitation.

He looked at his mum, who twitched her head towards the door. A silent instruction that he should leave. He did as requested without another word. Once more, it was the two sisters.

'I was so jealous when you had him, Sue,' Laura admitted, her voice wavering. 'I thought, 'course it's our Sue who had the boy. Now …' The truth hung between them.

'I know.' It was all Susan could say.

'I'm glad it's you that's doing it.' Laura took her sister's hands in her own and kissed them. 'Come on, sis. Standing here crying isn't what we're about.'

Matching steps, the two women left the room and headed towards the basement. Liam never said a word when his mum returned alone. He put a pillow over his head to block out her wails when she showered. He missed his dad.

6.

Birthday Presents

'I CAN'T EAT any more. I'm stuffed,' Liam moaned as another plate was put in front of him by his wife.

'Come on, babe,' Julie asked softly. 'Me and your mum have worked hard on this all afternoon.'

Groaning dramatically, Liam picked up the fork and ate the meat in front of him. It was his third plate.

'I won't make my nineteenth birthday if you guys keep feeding me like this.' He laughed.

'I've seen you eat double this after a workout.' Julie laughed.

Susan came out the kitchen and put a drink in front of her son.

'One or two more bites at least. Then you need to drink this.' Her tone was one of no argument. Liam watched her exchange a look with Julie and forced another mouthful.

He pushed the plate away to signify he couldn't carry on.

'Why didn't you two have anything? You made all this food, and only I got to eat it.' He thought he knew but didn't want to probe too deeply. Neither answered him.

'Drink up, Susan reminded him with a waving of her hand.

He did as he was told. He always did as he was told. It was how he had been raised. Wiping his mouth with the back of his hand, he let out a belch.

'And I am done!' He laughed.

Julie took his plate away. Susan nodded once more as Julie walked past and shut the door.

'Happy Birthday again, son,' Susan started. 'You're officially a man now.'

Liam changed position in his chair; something about his mother's tone made him feel uncomfortable.

'Your father would be so proud of the person you've become.' Liam opened his mouth to speak, but a stern hand from his mother froze the words in his throat. 'You are, as you know, the first male born into our family in so many years, we thought that it would never happen. But here you are.' Susan paused; with a shaking hand, she took a sip of wine from the glass that had sat before her all evening. 'There are certain beliefs in our family. You've had to be protected from them because everything that happens now is beyond your control.'

Liam's mouth was dry. The door clicked open as Julie came back in. She walked round the table and stood behind him. She put a hand on his shoulder, and he reached for it.

'This isn't going to be easy to hear, but we've all known since your birth that this is where we would end up.'

'You're freaking me out a little, Mum,' Liam confessed. He felt Julie's hand squeeze his shoulder.

'You, Liam, have to carry on this family legacy. Small though the family is now.' Susan paused, taking another sip of wine and forcing the memories of her family from her mind. 'You are going to have all the gifts this family have. You will pass these on to your children. They will pass it to their children, and so on. Until another son is born.'

Liam looked upward at his wife. She looked so young from this angle. They were both so young. There were no plans of a baby yet. They hadn't even been allowed to sleep in the same room since their wedding day.

'Mum, seriously …'

'We've collected the gifts we could. Languages from your aunt, artistry from your grandfather, words from your cousin. Do you understand?' her voice pleaded with him.

'Not really,' he confessed.

'You're currently full of strength from your father.' The words hung in the air for a moment.

Liam looked at the plate before him. The grey meat sat in a puddle of greasy fat.

'What?' His stomach churned. 'Are you joking?'

'No.' A single word.

It was all it took. He could feel his body repelling the meal he had so enjoyed.

'I'm sorry it has to be like this, Liam.' His mother's eyes brimmed with tears. 'Always remember that I love you. I've always loved you.' Liam started to stand up. 'Everything I've done has been for this moment.'

Chimera

He felt a sharp scratch on the side of his neck. His suddenly woozy eyes looked at his wife as she removed the syringe from his skin.

'You will be the best of this family.' His mother's words sounded far away as he fell into a darkness.

7.

Legacy

LIAM STRUGGLED TO open his eyes. They felt so heavy. His body was a map of agony. His tongue felt too big for his mouth. He wanted to lift his hands, but they also weighed more than he remembered.

'He's waking up.'

He recognised the voice as Julie's. He felt a cool hand stroke his hair as he started to drift back into the slumber.

'Liam?' It was his mother's voice. Heavy eyelids lifted. He saw her concerned face come into his blurred line of vision. 'Help him up,' she ordered Julie.

His wife did as she was told. Liam groaned as he sat up. His vision was returning to him. His mouth was on fire. He tried to speak and couldn't form any words. He tried to lift his arm to his face.

The scream that escaped him ripped his throat raw.

He had an extra set of hands on each arm.

'Shhhhh,' his mum tried to soothe.

'Baby, please.' Julie's voice joined the attempt.

His hands made their way to the pain in his mouth. All four of his hands jerked back when they felt the second tongue that was hanging out of his mouth. Another scream escaped him. His vision blacked out as he slumped backwards.

'Liam?' Julie shook her husband.

'He's passed out,' Susan stated.

'What now?' Julie asked her mother-in-law.

'Now? We wait. When he next comes round, we'll have to show him the new him.' Susan's own voice wavered. 'I wish I could have prepared him,' she confessed in a whisper.

'Me too. I've felt so bad keeping this from him.'

'He's still my beautiful boy, though.' Susan ran a hand across her son. He had his cousin's hands. His aunt's tongue. His grandfather's eyes. 'He's the tapestry of our family now, Julie.'

She broke down. Eighteen years of gathering his birthday presents.

'He'll make a wonderful father,' Susan told her daughter-in-law.

'I think so,' Julie admitted.

She just hoped that when the time came, she had a daughter.

James Lefebure

Aberdeen born, Liverpool living author who has been a fan of the horror genre since his first Goosebumps book back in the '80s.

Can often be found trading at comic cons, horror cons, and comic markets. Or reading horror and forcing his long-suffering partner to watch *Candyman* because "it's a romance movie, really!"

Firm believer that Jason would absolutely beat Michael in a fight!

BUILT FOR TWO
Tom Anderson

WAKE UP.

GET OUT OF BED, YOU PIECE OF MEAT.

THAT'S RIGHT.

LISTEN TO ME.

IT'S THE ONLY WAY YOU'LL EVER HAVE PEACE.

YOU SEE, WE'RE JOINED TOGETHER YOU AND I.

FROM THE BEGINNING TILL THE END.

THE BITTERSWEET END.

The voice inside our head was a little bit louder and angrier than usual this morning.

We look over to the bedside table and see the array of drugs, carefully placed into a small paper cup by the nurse this morning.

Wednesday.

Haloperidol, Thioradazine, Citalopram, Duloxetine.

Water laced with electrolytes in case of almost certain reactionary oral expulsion. The medical names are fixed in our mind, this is standard procedure and has been for a long time.

AT LEAST WE KNOW IT ENDS SOON.

WE FINISH EVERYTHING.

Today is family therapy with Mum.

Momma bear.

Mother dearest.

BRINGER OF LIFE.

OUR BEGINNING.

Chimera

Monday is CBT & Group therapy.

Tuesday is a reflective day.

Wednesday is Family therapy.

Thursday is Psychodynamic theory.

Friday is Dialectical Behaviourism treatment.

Saturday is Holistic Meditation.

Sunday is Transactional Analysis and Gestalt Systemic Treatment.

We have memorised these days; it has been so long.

Twenty-five years.

TWENTY-FIVE LONG YEARS.

ALL LEADING TO THIS.

TODAY IS THE DAY.

Our white room has a canvas bed, itchy blanket, stiff pillow and a hard steel bedside table with medicine and fracture-proof plastic glass perched on top.

All kept at a perfectly regulated seventy degrees F.

No more, no less.

Year in, year out.

BANAL ISN'T IT?

NO ESCAPE.

No seasons except through the window in the common area.

IT'S TODAY YOU KNOW.

IT WILL HAPPEN TODAY.

We know.

Our birthday.

HAPPY BIRTHDAY TO US.

We take the medicine and gulp the fluid, nodding our head to cement the thought quicker within ourselves.

It calcifies, imbuing hatred and rage within our vessels.

We cannot let it show. That would defeat everything. We would be sedated and strapped. Kept away for life.

YES, IT WILL HAPPEN.

IMAGINE EVERY GLORIOUS MOMENT.

REMEMBER TO SAVOUR.

The thought momentarily sends electric pleasure through our body, making our fingers quiver and arm hairs arise.

We look in the mirror. A gaunt and wiry being with sandy blonde hair, shorn down to a standard number 1 cut all over the scalp. Pale, electric blue eyes pierce back at us with an echoing ethereal fury.

A toothy grin forms.

'Happy Birthday,' we say into the mirror.

Forty-five years young today.

CALM DOWN.

LISTEN TO ME.

I HAVE NEVER PUT YOU WRONG SO FAR.

I AM YOUR BOLSTER.

The grin dropped, turning into a smile intending to display calmness and serenity.

NICELY DONE.

BE THE PERFECT MODEL OF A REFORMED PATIENT.

THEY WILL BE HERE SOON.

The door in the room opened, and a nurse waved them through past the common area; still foetid with mass-production meals and UHT milk for general population patients.

It was sunny. Clear skies as far as they could see. There would be birds singing in the trees if we could hear them past the muted and sealed windows.

IMAGINE BEING FREE FROM HERE.

THE WIND ON OUR ARMS.

THE SMELL OF FRESH AIR.

WHAT A PITY.

We pass a locked steel door and into a similar, smaller white room with a table and 3 chairs.

We sit down.

The door shut.

SOON.

VERY SOON.

PATIENCE IS A VIRTUE.

Time passed.

The door opposite opened, and through it walked a therapist with Mum in tow.

THERE SHE IS.

The therapist is a soft and flabby man, greying at the temples, wearing a muted-coloured plaid shirt, faded blue jeans, and shabby moccasins.

Dr. Gready.

He speaks with a soft lilting and poignant accent intended to bring empathy, but instead brings pretension and braggadociousness.

WE KNOW WHAT HE WANTS TO HEAR.

WE'VE REHEARSED THIS TIME AFTER TIME AFTER TIME.

PUT IT INTO PLAY.

Mum is wearing her usual attire. A long black dress with a subtle grey flower pattern. Her ivory white hair swept back into a tight ponytail. The flat canvas shoes on her feet sound as if she is wearing high heels with the immediacy that her gait brings. A long grey cardigan to cover the track marks.

RELAX.

IT'S SIMPLY ANOTHER DAY.

IT'S JUST OUR LAST DAY.

Gready's soft voice breaks the silence.

"Hello Luke"

WELL, THAT'S RUDE.

HE NEVER SAYS HELLO TO ME.

HE NEVER EVEN LOOKED UP FROM HIS NOTES.

"I believe last week we spoke about the importance of honesty. Reflecting on that…."

Gready's eyes turned upwards.

'Is there anything you would like to bring forward today?'

LOOK AT HER.

LOOK IN HER BLOODSHOT EYES.

SHE'S SHAKING.

SHE'S EITHER HIGH OR COMING DOWN.

LOOK AT HER SWEATING BULLETS.

'Don't think so.'

THAT'S RIGHT.

ACT CASUAL.

STAY STILL.

BE CALM.

'Things have actually been really good the last few months.'

LIE TO HIM.

BRING HIM FALSE HOPE.

MAKE HIM FEEL COMFORTABLE.

'I know this is usually a difficult time of year, but there really has been progress made.'

WELL DONE.

HE LOOKS IMPRESSED.

LOOK AT HIM, SURVEYING THE NOTES HE HAS SEEN SO MANY FUCKING TIMES BEFORE.

AS IF ANYTHING NEW WILL BE THERE.

Gready's voice crackled past the momentary silence.

'That's fantastic. I can see here that regular intensive treatment is doing wonders. Frequent voluntary inclusion with group activities alongside a vast improvement in incident reports. I believe that in the very near future you may not be here anymore.'

HAH.

THE IRONY.

IF ONLY HE KNEW.

In the other chair; pulled away from us, Mum is rhythmically shaking, her face buried in a handkerchief.

'Jane, is there anything you'd like to mention?'

SHE'S NOT HERE.

SHE NEVER IS.

SHE IS THE REASON.

SHE IS WHY WE'RE HERE.

BECAUSE OF HER.

BECAUSE OF HER ADDICTION.

BECAUSE OF HER FUCKING NEGLECT.

She raises her head slightly.

'It's your birthday, you know.'

Her cracked voice is heavy with tobacco as tears seeped out from her wrinkled eyes.

Her arms trembled.

Her veins stuck out like ropes amongst the blue bruises and needle marks.

A momentary guttural sob.

'Daisy… daisy………give me your answer do……. I'm half crazy……all for the love of you……….. You'll look sweet……upon the seat….. of a bicycle built for two.'

THAT FUCKING SONG.

EVERY DAY.

EVERY HOUR.

IT IS HER MANTRA.

WE HEARD IT ALWAYS.

EVERY MINUTE.

EVERY MOMENT.

FOR YEARS.

UNTIL WE HAD TO REACT.

UNTIL WE HAD TO RETALIATE.

AND THEN SHE PUT US HERE.

STAY CALM.

PUT THE PLAN INTO ACTION.

A momentary silence pierced the room.

'Sorry Dr. Gready, would it be at all possible to have some water?'

'Of course.' A button on the underside of the table is pressed.

'May we have some water brought to therapy Room 4, please?'

Moments pass and a light buzz of noise emerges from a tiny speaker.

'Two minutes.' A metallic voice responds.

NOW.

GO.

DO IT.

AIM FOR JUST ABOVE HER CLAVICLE.

CRUSH IT WITH YOUR THUMBS.

FEEL THE BLOOD VESSELS POP BETWEEN YOUR FINGERS.

LISTEN TO HER GURGLE FOR AIR.

We stand, slowly.

We make a fake gesture of stretching out leg discomfort. A reason for us to stand upright without causing alarm.

We look at Dr. Gready, who matches our eye contact.

We make a silent gesture after a few seconds, lead by our hands, eyes, and head as if to say 'Is it alright if I hug her?'

A moment passes.

It felt like an eternity.

This is strictly not allowed, but these moments of growth, this display of apathy; surely this is a turning point. These are the thoughts running through Gready's mind.

He nods, attentively.

We move slowly.

Carefully.

EITHER THAT OR BRING A KNEE INTO HER NOSE.

THEN SLAM HER MOUTH AND TEETH INTO THE BENCH.

LISTEN TO THE CRUNCH.

THEN AS SHE FALLS, YOU DRIVE THE HEEL OF YOUR FOOT INTO THE BACK OF HER NECK, AS MANY TIMES AS YOU CAN.

IDEALLY UNTIL YOU FEEL THE FRACTURED BONES OF HER SKULL IN BETWEEN YOUR TOENAILS.

'It's all your fault you know.' Mother's voice injected the room.

WHAT?

WHAT DID SHE FUCKING SAY?

SAY THAT A-FUCKING-GAIN.

We freeze in step.

'We had to move house. We had to change jobs. We had to uproot everything before you were born. Your father was so happy. I was so happy. A family. So soon.'

The room turned cold in an instant.

'My first scan. I was so young. We didn't know what to expect.'

Bile and wrath emerged in our throat alongside the sickening taste of Blackcurrant Dioralyte.

'Twins. Two beautiful babies. A girl. A boy.'

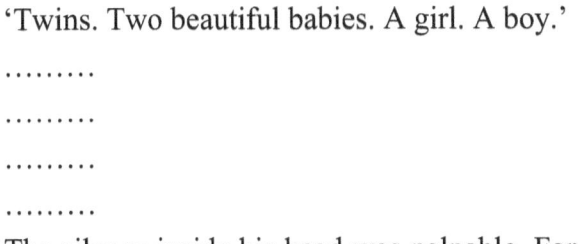

The silence inside his head was palpable. For the first time in his life.

No noise.

No echo.

No voice.

No instruction.

Emptiness.

'We had to find two of everything. Two cribs. Two bottles. Two lots of clothes. One baby pink. One sky blue. Daisy. After his mother. And you. Lucas. Named after my father.'

The room began to vibrate inside of his mind, a high-pitched squeal intersecting the empty noise in the room. A sickening haze fell.

'We had everything planned. We went on holiday to celebrate. We were foolish and thought that everything was fine. We didn't go back to the hospital until I was in labour.'

He had to sit down.

His knees weakened and his spirits flushed.

Everything controlling him had vanished.

'Then you emerged after six hours. Just you.'

The space he was in appeared distorted, a wash of unfamiliar shapes and frequencies.

With no one there to control, he was empty.

'You. You'd eaten your sister. Enveloped her. Killed her. Inside of me. I had contractions for another 8 hours even after you had been delivered.'

At that moment a loud snap in his mind.

A click that felt like a lock falling into place on a bank vault door.

The thick grey blanket of fog dissipated.

He looked into his mother's pale and bloodshot eyes.

Things were perfectly clear now.

'Your father. He couldn't accept it. He couldn't look at you without hating you. He sang that song as he slashed his arms open from his wrists up to his elbows and bled out in front of me...... because of you...... because of Daisy.....'

SORRY ABOUT THAT.

HAD A MOMENT THERE DIDN'T WE?

AT LEAST WE KNOW MY NAME NOW.

DAISY.

THE PLEASURE IS ALL MINE.

NOW.

GO.

The haze now gone, we bolted forward, a flash of energy and an explosion of force brought us onto her.

Almost immediately the sirens burst out from the speakers in the room, blasting violent sonic sounds across the ward.

We land our first blow, a right knuckle into her orbital bone. We hear a crack under their fist. Blood flew onto the white walls of the room and aqueous humour splashed on our hand. A skin-crawling scream emanated.

We sing together now; for the first time in our lives.

It was in perfect harmony.

A beautiful song of old.

'DDAaIiSsYy DdAaIiSsYy'

ANOTHER.

Our left elbow found its way into her ribs. A dull crunch echoed into her body. The scream from the first blow was now almost completely silenced by a wet agonising thud.

'GgIiVvEe MmEe YyOoUuRr AaNnSsWwEeRr DdOo'

ANOTHER.

Our knee found its way into her nose as she fell lumbering to the floor. A sickening noise emerged from her face, a snap of cartilage and torn ligaments.

'WWEe'RrEe…'

ANOTHER.

A quick, furious slap landed across her face as an insult to injury as she lay on the floor. Not unlike the ones we got growing up for not doing what we were told.

'HHAaLlFf CcRrAaZzYy'

ANOTHER.

A lightning-fast jab erupted into the side of her jaw, swinging it open like a door in the wind. Molars, incisors, and darkened cavity-filled teeth flew across the sparse space.

'AaLl FfOoRr TtHhEe LlOoVvEe OoFf YyOoUu'

ANOTHER.

We cradle her head now, our right forearm under her chin, nestling together with their left arm in an unbreakable knot, mingled with her knotted hair and sweating brow.

We can feel her softly breathing now. We can feel her pain. Our grip slowly but viciously tightens.

'WWEe'Ll LlOoKk SsWwEeTt'

We feel the warm fluid of her blood and saliva run down their forearm.

We hear now the multitude of armoured nurses, stomping echoes marching down the hall towards the therapy room.

'UuPpOoNn TtHhEe SsEeAaTt'

For the first time that we could remember we kiss our mother. We plant our lips upon her bloodied face and gave a big juicy smooch.

'OoFf Aa BbliCcYyCcLlEe BbUuliLlTt FfOoRr…………

……..ONE?!'

HAH. 'Hah.'

HAHAHA. 'Hahaha.'

AAHAHAHAHA. 'Aahahahaha.'

'Hahahaha hahahaha!'

snap

They are here now.

The armed response with riot shields.

It didn't matter.

We let go of her.

She slumped like a ragdoll.

We embrace what would happen.

Upwards we stand, our arms out wide in acceptance.

We look at Gready, hidden cowering in the corner.

'You read what.........WE did years ago. Sorry you had to see the encore. You have to admit though, she deserved every second of pain.'

The door came off its hinges.

We hear our last sounds in these moments.

Our mother's last breath echoed past our ears, soft, moist, and gentle. Full of blood and sweat.

All juxtaposed with a cacophony of batons crushing our skull, bringing the blissful silence of death.

It was a sound sweeter than anything they had heard before.

Tom Anderson

This is Tom Anderson's first ever story.

Even though he has been telling them for years as a GM of RP games (GURPS, D&D, Pathfinder, etc), this is the first one that he has written for more than the people present in the room at the time.

If you enjoyed this, Tom's debut novel, Cornucopia, is available now. Imagine if the films Se7en and 8MM had a baby, and you'll have the gist.

THREE
Astrid Addams

An introduction by Astrid Addams

According to our modern god, otherwise known as Google: A libertine is basically someone who thinks for themselves, unconstrained by what they are meant to think. They are free thinking, thinking outside religious, social, and moral constraints. They are also someone who does not care for what is right or morally wrong but does what they want regardless.

"Three" is a modernised and very condensed retelling of de Sade's novel 120 Days of Sodom. *We shouldn't forget that at certain points in history, atheism, paedophilia, and being gay were considered on a similar level of deviance. But I have given/changed certain characteristics, either because they are missing in action or because they are inadequate or just because this is my story and I'll mutilate whomever I choose. I have added a feminist agenda and perspective on the many women in the text. Because I simply do not believe that the Brothel keepers (as de Sade refers to them) and the other female hardened criminals would put up with de Sade's libertine's shit. Especially when it becomes apparent, as it does in the original text, that their own hides are at risk.*

In hindsight, I feel that the Marquis de Sade wrote 120 Days of Sodom *as a satire of the rich and powerful. Feel free to google it, hell, even check out the original part-constructed novel, if you have a strong enough stomach. That is, if you get through my own stomach-churning creation.*

Trigger Warning: This story may not be for the weaker stomached. It also contains subject matter that the reader may find disturbing, offensive, or grotesque, such as blasphemy, references to sexual abuse, torture, and coprophagia.

IT SHOULD HAVE been a mansion, or maybe a white palace, like in the Disney pornos her father had made her watch when she was small. But it wasn't. Aline guessed that such things were far too indiscreet and luxurious for the libertines' purposes. They weren't really free thinkers, after all; *The Human Centipede Part 2* had taken place in a warehouse. They were just some sick old men with too much money and time, blowing each other's egos just as they blew each other. Telling themselves that they and their 'passions' were 'unique' and 'original.' Aline knew otherwise, yet she had no choice but to go along with their games and 'experiments.' She had been conceived and allowed to be born for their amusement and to do their bidding; not doing so resulted in the type of punishments Aline continued to have nightmares about. That was why she'd been let out of her cage, to do what they said. She was only ever taken out of her cage to amuse her father or to be punished in new and imaginative ways. Like the time he took her to the beach and made her watch the other kids play and laugh in the sand and the sea whilst he drove pins into her clitoris.

This time, they were in a dirty warehouse on a derelict industrial estate, miles from anywhere.

"Where no one can hear them scream." Her father The Bishop, so called because of his position in the church and his deep love of buggering altar boys, had laughed to his brother, who had driven her and her sister Julie to this dump in his luxury car.

Bored and anxious, Aline and Julie stood in their thin Grecian sheet dresses that barely covered anything and waited, squeezing each other's hands as the game's other participants were led into the room by the masked men. Over the heads of the trembling boys and girls, Aline stared at the twisted figure in black stood at the other end of the room. Cloudy, runny eyes, red around the edges, stared at her, the white of her bald head in stark contrast to the gloom of the shadows. Aline gritted her teeth; she might be about to become some old man's—hell, maybe even her father's— bitch for a solid *four months*, but she had been thankful that at least she would be escaping *her*. That whatever humiliations she would be subjected to, at least Terese wouldn't witness it!

They were soon joined by the usual suspects. Constance, looking plumper and paler than normal in a matching toga, greeted Aline with a hug and kiss of friendship, which they both knew would be broken and betrayed for their fathers' and husbands' amusement. Adelade managed a small smile through the choke marks on her neck. Being a fervent Christian, Adelade received the most abuse from their fathers, who fancied themselves free thinkers, partly because they didn't *believe*. Aline had often wondered if it wasn't Adelade, tortured and surrounded by cruelty and mockery yet refusing to give up her faith, who was the real free thinker.

Constance was by far the strongest of the four daughters. Aline knew that and envied her strength and kindness in the face of extreme pain and cruelty. If anyone was suited to be married to her uncle the Duc, it was Constance. Constance approached the children—each wore little white togas with nothing underneath and large name badges—and listened to the sobs and sorry tales of kidnap, murder, and intimate physical examinations. All except for the small girl with hair far redder than blood, so red in fact, Aline was sure it couldn't be natural. The girl's label said Rossette, and she stood apart from the other children gathered around Constance as if she was embarrassed by their tears. Rossette's blue eyes met Aline's; the girl glanced at the others and rolled her eyes. Uncomfortable, Aline turned to watch the other strangers arrive, all adults entering the warehouse in groups. Aline allowed herself to look away from Terese as she roamed among the kids, a vulture among a flock of pink flamingo chicks and one red cuckoo.

Led in first was a group of three very dirty, decrepit old women who stumbled into the room, cackling madly together.

They must be the servants of some sort, thought Aline, looking at their age and deformities. *Or maybe a joke from the President.*

The President had to be one of the sickest people she'd ever met, and her father subjected her to the most depraved freaks he could find. The President was the corpse-fucking—not just any corpse, no, *rotten corpse*-fucking—anal-raping, shit-eating lover of everything ugly and abominable rolled into one politician. He was now her brother-in-law! All because of Julie's rotten teeth and refusal to shower or treat her BO! Aline looked furtively at her sister, who swayed where they stood together, drunk at eleven in the morning! Aline was pissed but couldn't blame her.

In a panic, Aline realised that *she* was gone. No longer snarling at any child who got too close nor staring disapproving daggers at Constance. Aline mentally cursed as she scanned the room, the shadows, Rossette examining Adelade, the old hags, the

56

eight men she'd never seen before who had just arrived and wore nothing but cod pieces. Gone. Frantic, Aline scanned again, finally spotting the old hag, now crouched beside the red-headed girl as if she was whispering in Rossette's ear. Terese looked up and leered at her, runny eyes focused in on her, and Aline looked away. But it was too late, the old woman's focus was once again upon her, and Aline squirmed helplessly under it.

Shouts of laughter disturbed Aline as the masked men led in four brilliantly dressed and made-up women, who chattered happily together. Aline frowned at Terese, who, she was pleased to see, was watching the women with a vindictive judgement twisted by age and insanity. Aline watched as the masked men left the room and heard the screaming of the locks as they were entombed together. Julie's nails dug into her arm like talons. Terese now stood beside Constance with her back to them, black rags fluffed out around her, staring into the shadows ahead.

Suddenly, the shadows were flooded with a brilliant light, illuminating four men in white robes that emerged from the darkness. Brown wigs and beards adorned each face. Behind them was a dead Black kid nailed to a crucifix, naked and with a huge bulbous and bloated erection. Words and symbols carved into his flesh blossomed with blood, now drying under the spot light. How original! Still, the kids and Adelade gave the reaction the libertines so desperately wanted. Aline heard the women behind laugh and whoop. Julie laughed beside her, and Aline kicked her shin as hard as she could without shoes. Julie hissed and clawed her back, then mutually avenged, as was their understanding, they waited together in the silence.

It was a thick silence, pregnant with threat, fear, and anticipation. The hairs at the back of Aline's neck stood up as she waited breathlessly to find out their fate, to know the odds of her going back to the dingy hovel her father kept her prisoner in with Terese. But the libertines lived for dragging misery out and weren't about to speak until the maximum tension had been built up. Now, Terese stood at her neck, her remaining long, twisted fingers, broken too many times to ever set straight, twisted in Aline's long light-brown hair. Her toothless mouth rasped wordlessly in her ears like spider webs. Aline was certain she was dying as the tongue of the woman, blue and rotten, a giant slug of decay, licked the back of her neck.

She knew what was going to happen; all the daughters did. Their fathers, now husbands, were going to big themselves up with their claims of superiority and how they all must obey their commands no matter what or face punishment. But that wasn't the end, oh no; the end was the torture and death of yourself or someone else and you being obliged to assist or die yourself. So why wasn't the libertines' show happening? What was different about today in this warehouse? Aline felt the difference the moment the libertines emerged, each one dressed as pornographic versions of Jesus. She sensed it in her scar tissue, the parts of her bones that had been broken and reset multiple times. In the constant irritation and trauma between her legs and inside her constantly torn and itching rectum. Where it niggled that something was happening outside the libertines' control. Terese's bark, millimetres from her ear, confirmed it just before one of the glamorous made-up women rose above the dirty concrete floor, levitating above them, her black gown billowing out around her as if the fabric was actually growing.

Blonde highlights swept up to defy gravity. Black gloves covered her hands and forearms. Her shoes, high-heeled and black with red soles, fell from what seemed to be nothingness as she rose higher and higher above them so that Aline had to lean her neck backwards to maintain her view of what had previously looked like a woman. Those who had not moved away from her space pushed back, creating a circle of darkness underneath the woman, whose smile was just a little too wide, her dress just a little too shiny, her makeup just a smidgen too thick.

'Ladies, gentlemen, victims,' the woman's voice, alive, cheerful, and full of humour, addressed them. 'For those who do not know, I go by the name of Duclos. Our four *honourable* hosts gathered you all here today so that we may enact an experiment for their *amusement*. My role was to be the first of four storytellers, detailing the *innocent* and *tedious* passions men such as our hosts consider *edgy* and are required to pay to indulge in.'

Aline's eyes stole to the stage, where her father and his friends stood staring out at Duclos, suddenly comical in their costumes. Aline had never seen anyone confront or go against her father and his friends, she suspected neither had they, but Aline was overjoyed at their obvious discomfort.

'Hey, Al, it looks like Daddy is going to choke,' Julie whispered gleefully. Her own father, for they only shared a mother, looked like some giant invisible hand was squeezing him. 'However, I am not going to enact my given role. But I am going to tell you a far more *interesting* story.' Duclos's skirts shifted as if the black satin was somehow alive.

'A very long time ago, when I myself was a pretty young whore of fifteen or sixteen, my Madam came to me to discuss a special request from a rich gentleman. As a great lover of money and overindulgence, I, of course, was intrigued, as the Madam knew I would be.

'The man was and continues to be a well-known sodomite with a preference for men,' Duclos continued. 'So I was even more intrigued to learn what he could possibly wish to pay me a substantial amount of money for.'

The woman's voice was hypnotic, and now the most sensual thing Aline had ever heard. No longer did she wonder about the libertines, who had suddenly become secondary characters in their own story. All that mattered was that Duclos continued with her narrative, which seemed to Aline to be vitally important.

'Madam sat me down on the fat overstuffed arm chair, left to her by a lifelong patron. It was a great honour to be permitted to sit on the thing. Madam sat opposite me, where I would have normally sat, and took my hands in hers, refusing to look me in the eye. I knew she felt ashamed of whatever she was going to ask of me.

'The Madam's shame intrigued me. What could possibly shame the woman who sold my virginity? Well, it was Mr Durcet over there's proposition. You see, the "accident" that killed his parents had resulted in a very large inheritance. So to celebrate, Mr Durcet went on an expedition to find and explore the most taboo and exotic pleasures this world has to offer, and he desired a woman to bear a child for him. Not his child or any man's, what Mr Durcet wanted was to see if a woman could bear and deliver the child of an abomination newly discovered in the waters of an unnamed island.'

Duclos's voice had become razor sharp. Her eyes, though dark, seemed illuminated as they focused on the libertines, particularly the investment banker Durcet. Not above taking other people's money to get what he wanted, Aline was convinced that the amount of money required to potentially acquire such a creature would be limitless. Durcet didn't look away at Duclos's confrontation; in fact, he stared back defiantly as Duclos smiled.

'Being a poor little thieving whore with expensive tastes and no rich family to murder, I agreed in exchange for a series of substantial payments.

'So, I was taken to a secret location, where I opened my legs so that the creature's seed could be squirted into me. It was cold and smelled of dead fish. It stung my insides as it slithered and *moved* through me. I knew it was wrong. Not morally, of course, morals are merely fairy tales. But every nerve down below my waist, right down to my toes, screamed out against the assault of that creature's spunk. But by God, I loved money and the drugs and the silks and the high-price booze and the finest women it could buy. So I laid there, my legs in the stirrups, screeching like a scalded cat as that stuff ate into me, not once nor twice but three times before I became pregnant.'

Aline felt sick, staring up at the levitating woman. She glanced at Constance, who herself was in the early stages of pregnancy with her rapist's child, possibly her own sibling. Constance was green; Adelade and Rossette practically held her up.

61

'It was an horrific but mercifully short pregnancy of everything I could ever want and constant care and attention. After five months, I gave birth, and the creature was rushed from between my legs by the doctors before I'd even caught sight of it. No matter, I may well have smothered it if it had been permitted to lay in my arms.' Still, Duclos smiled. To Aline, her hair had not just come loose but darkened and thickened as it flew around her head like Medusa's snakes.

'The baby gone, my service was over, and I was paid the remaining money and taken back to the establishment I had come from. I didn't stay, of course. I moved to accommodation suitable for a wealthy young thing and enjoyed the money and depravity it afforded me for two whole years before it ran out. Then life continued as I had always expected when my Madam welcomed me back with open arms.

'Except for one thing—dull aches and pains began to plague me every so often, as if my soul, somewhere far below in hell, was being tormented. I went to every doctor and took every concoction, but still the unpleasant sensations continued. Up until five years ago, when I was forty and other *changes* took over.'

Duclos's tone remained light hearted, but Aline shivered and found her eyes wandering the crowd. There was Terese, beside her father, her back to Aline, her scalp reflecting the light back out at the crowd. She could tell by her posture that the old bitch was snarling in his face.

'Whilst at Mr Durcet's house a few days ago, when the man was intoxicated past the point of no return, Durcet disclosed some information to me for the first time. The infant had been female and had provided him a great deal of entertainment until she died five years ago, when the nagging sensations that had plagued me for decades mysteriously vanished. When I myself began to … *evolve.*'

Duclos's long black skirts began to unravel and drop, no longer mere fabric but metamorphosed with her words into thick, black, shiny, slimy flesh that rolled and danced in the air above their heads as they unravelled, blocking out the harsh lighting in a sea of thick tar.

'Now, gentlemen,' Duclos's voice rang out somewhere above them. 'Whilst myself and my colleagues planned to steal everything we could from you and cut your stubbled throats, I propose a more interesting and *fun* idea.'

Terese was beside Aline in the darkness, remaining crooked fingers entwined in Aline's. The woman she hated, who was her only companion, sometimes for months at a time, held her tightly as screams tore through the darkness and blood rained down upon their heads. It was blood; Aline recognised the copper tang in the air and on her skin as Terese licked it from her face like a dog, except with worse breath. Aline was blinded by a sudden light just as the red rain began to slow and slowly stop. Adelade screamed nearby, and Aline felt the strong urge to smack her pure, righteous face as, vulnerable in the sudden light, she blinked furiously before finding herself able to see the massacre around them.

The men in jock straps were dead, twisted and broken into ambitious modern art structures of unspeakable horror. The former mistresses of rape and the old women were nothing more than a lumpy thick coating on the walls, floor, and ceiling in the vague area where they had stood only minutes before. The libertines, all but the well-known coward the Duc, stood on stage, their costumes drenched in blood but otherwise unharmed. Duclos hovered above them, licking blood from the thick, black appendages where her hands and arms should be.

Aline heard the frantic callings of the other daughters as the libertines, seizing their chance, dashed from the stage. Adelade and Constance were rounding up the children, and Julie was stumbling around, trying to help them.

'It's time.' Terese's voice sounded almost like Duclos's. Aline half believed that if she looked behind at the woman, she would have Duclos's face.

But Aline didn't look around to find out. Instead, she propelled herself forwards and around the stage, then through the doorway the libertines had deserted them through. Aline hurried down the corridor, flimsy white fabric, cooling and clammy, clinging to her skin—half expecting the door she'd followed them through to fly open at any minute and Julie to chase after her and drag her back to the other daughters and the brats. Her breath forced itself from her lungs as if it was herself who had just been broken. Her father would have fled the building and left them to die; Aline was certain of that. Her only hope was that whatever measures the libertines had put in place to stop their prisoners from escaping and prevent thieves now held the libertines captive. In which case, her father would be hiding somewhere he thought was clever.

Aline crouched behind a rusting cabinet and tried to think clearly. A metal shard, sharp and small enough to conceal in her hands, called to her from the grimy floor. Gingerly, it found its way between her fingers. Trying not to breathe, Aline listened, then peered out from her hiding place. Nothing and no one were there, only the stillness and dread, far worse than any pain, man, or monsters.

Cautiously, Aline began to creep down the corridor, doing her best to listen and prepare herself. This, after all, was what she'd wanted for a long time, the opportunity she'd never thought she'd get. Aline stopped. The black grime in front of her, about an arm's length away, was smudged, as if something or someone had been dragged away. There didn't seem to be any blood; hopefully, that meant life.

Tense with anxiety, Aline peered around the corner. The smudge continued towards a fire exit, then off to the left, where Aline found a door with a wooden crucifix nailed to it.

This must be the toilets, Aline thought, shaking her head.

Her hand squeezed the metal shard as she crept forwards, ignoring the obvious Fire Exit trap and the severed fingers lying on the floor in their own little puddle.

'Good, now it's tasted blood. The edge will be hungrier now!' Terese hissed beside her as Aline's other hand pushed the bathroom door open. Fear, terror, and excitement of who and what might be hiding beyond held her.

'Come on, girl, take a look,' cackled Terese. 'You have to see this!'

Slowly, Aline peeked beyond the door. Lying on what Adelade might call an "alter" was Durcet. Still in his tacky Jesus costume, now red with his own blood. The coppery smell assaulted Aline's nose, but she held her breath, refusing to cough or choke. Why should she choke just because his friends had gouged his eyes out? Scooped his heart right out of his chest and set it inside the gold bed pan next to a pile of shit. A fresh pile of shit, still warm and tempting a swarm of flies away from the crude holes where Durcet's leering eyes had been.

Aline continued around the "alter" into what was actually a fully functional communal bathroom, except the stall doors had been removed and graphic blasphemous works of art adorned the walls. Some designed that way by the artists, some masterpieces vandalised and corrupted by her father and the President themselves. Why such things amused the libertines, Aline would never know. It was all familiar to her, from Jesus shitting out communion wafers for the Christians below to eat to God, who always looked like one of the libertines, raping the Virgin Mary. The pain on the girl's face had distressed Aline when she was a young girl; now, she barely glanced at it as she continued the search for her father.

Past the artwork and the 'God is Dead' slogans daubed in shit. Heart hammering painfully in her chest, playing a symphony of pain on her scarred and chipped rib cage. Still, she gripped her shard between her bleeding and frequently dislocated fingers and crept on, through the puddles of piss, past her father's "The Rape of Jesus" portrait.

Her ears pricked, following the sounds of human whimpering that grew louder the further she crept into the stinking den. Aline, like most people, hated the smell and taste of bodily secretions. It was her misfortune that the Bishop and his friends loved it. Especially when it shocked, repulsed, or horrified their current harem. Now it worked to Aline's advantage, as the stench prevented her breathing and the persistent buzzing of the black flies camouflaged what little noises she did make. It was only the keen hearing she had developed as a child, listening out for her father and his friends' footsteps in the night, praying that it wouldn't be her turn to be tortured ... The libertines, Aline knew, had never known any real pain or suffering and never expected it would ever happen to them. They'd never learnt to hide or be cautious or quiet. As she got closer to the whimpering, somewhere nearby, someone else fought for every laboured breath they could take. It was a familiar sound to Aline. She didn't care if it was the President or the Duc or one of the masked men. But it had better not be the Bishop.

At last, she found her father, whimpering in the 'Abortion' cubicle, covered in blood, muttering to himself. His pale eyes were wild as they searched everywhere, including the backs of their own sockets. He didn't see Aline as she stood before him, wearing the revealing, now soaked costume the libertines had made their daughters wear. Aline stared at him. Her own eyes, pale like his, beamed her hate out at him like a laser, doing her best to make his head explode next to the toilet with just her hatred alone. Her eyes ached, her cheeks burnt with the effort.

'You like that, don't you?' Terese smirked, leaning against the remains of a sink. 'Seeing him suffer.'

That's when Aline realised that she had been grinning as the nearby death rattle faded out and died and was replaced by far more interesting sounds.

'Al ... ine?' the Bishop stuttered. His trembling, disgusting little hand, bleeding from the stumps where three of his fingers had once been, grabbed her empty hand and pulled her towards him.

Aline screamed—well, it was more a roar of rage and war that her father dared to touch her now. After himself and the libertines had been defeated, he still *dared* to touch her after everything he'd done to her and everything he'd forced her to do to others. He was a stupid, weak little man with spoilt masterpieces who was nothing without the protection of his money and status. He had never shown Aline or anyone else a single kindness or mercy, yet the man who'd taken great joy in anally raping her and forcing her to watch happy children play on the beach, who had never known anything like her pain, now expected kindness and mercy from her! Aline hadn't believed it possible to hate her father even more.

Looking down at him, hearing the siren of her own suffering bounce off the walls of the cubicle, Aline discovered she had been wrong as her other arm brought the shard, baptised with her own blood, down onto his face and head. And she just kept carving, ignoring his screams, kicks, scratches, and convulsions. Not caring if Duclos, the President, nor her uncle the Duc heard their last altercation. Nothing could save, nor anyone recognise, her father as his face, that he'd forced her to look at, became nothing but a bone-splintered crater. His screams became gurgles as his nose was severed and caved in, his lips and teeth shattered, his own death rattle struggling through as he choked on the remains of his own tongue. Even when he was nothing more than just another corpse, Aline kept going, ignoring the pain in her hands and throat. Until something cold took her hand, the one that housed her shard.

Spinning around, Aline found Terese gone. In her place levitated Duclos, smiling at her through her own bloody war paint.

Aline had never seen anything more beautiful, from the black tentacles to the mismatched eyes—one human, rich and dark, the other purple and bulging like a breathing amethyst.

~~~~

'Come, my sweet Aline.' Duclos smiled with multiple rows of shark teeth. 'Let's go and see what remains of their silly game.'

A sharp pain lit up Aline's hand. Looking down, she was shocked to discover the slab of raw meat that had once been her hand, most of the skin and some of the flesh flayed away by the rusty metal. Down to the bone in places, flesh and tendons pulsed beside bone. Despite the pain and a particularly large slice that pumped black blood out at her where her chunk of metal seemed to have *impaled* itself, Aline gritted her teeth and tried to bend her remaining finger. Barely a movement, only the realization that she had made a vital step and one that took her closer to Terese.

Pain was nothing new, and Aline accepted without complaint the burning medical alcohol and staples Duclos inserted into the remaining mess. Once her hand had been wrapped in clean bandages, Duclos offered Aline the black appendage where one of her tanned arms had once been. Spitting on the remains of the Bishop, Aline took it, and together, they left the dead meat. As they traversed arm in arm, as elegant as any couple can be, given the circumstances, Duclos spoke, but Aline didn't listen. She didn't need to hear the woman's words of praise and admiration to recognise the tone.

'I have always dreamt of meeting and wooing a woman of your beauty and intelligence, who will violently avenge themselves when the time comes.' Duclos smiled. 'It is not as common as you might imagine, especially with my current deformities.'

'You look awesome to me,' Aline murmured and was delighted when the part-human beside her kissed her cheek.

'I know.'

The grimy corridor passed them by as they got closer to the main room, where suddenly, the shouts and screams broke into Aline's consciousness. She began to run, pulling Duclos along behind her, heart in her throat. How could she have been selfish enough to leave Julie and Constance? Fear yanked at her with visions of the Duc bearing down upon them and the children, blood pouring from his lips as he devoured them, his *unholy* erection in hand. Wanting to scream herself, Aline hurled herself at the door, falling through it to her knees in front of the President, who was brandishing a sawed-off shotgun at Adelade's face. Duclos was the only thing preventing her from falling flat on her face before the surprised company.

'Can I help, Constance?' whispered a small voice.

Constance didn't speak but grabbed Adelade as Julie lurched for Aline herself.

'Why of course, Rossette, do your worst,' Aline heard Duclos call to the child as she found herself in Julie's arms as the shotgun roared and the young girl vanished. Not a slow horror film transformation but an immediate change in size, figure, and consistency as *extreme* details clicked into place.

Aline watched, eyes wide, as whiskers popped out of the yellow lion's face, mane-less but snarling down at the President. The most important man in the country lay at *hooved* feet. The shotgun shook in his hands, too much for him to reload it as a large green tail, scaly and ridged like a crocodile's, shot from amidst the shaggy hair of her backside.

Where Rossette had stood was a living cockatrice, stood over the President, regarding him as a low growl emitted from its throat. Without warning, a wave of fire shot from its mouth and engulfed the President. For once, it was him screaming in agony as his flesh roasted, his malevolent eyes melting backwards into their sockets.

Julie and the other daughters shepherded the crying children away from the horrific sight. But Aline, Duclos, and Rossette watched the flames until the President's bones began to pop in the ashes. Now the monster was gone, and Rossette stood before them, her whiskers retreating back into her face.

'Where are—?' Constance called from where she tried to shield the children.

'Dead, dead, and deader still.' Duclos smiled. 'What remains of them are in the bathroom, if you'd like to pay your respects?'

'Can I go home now?' Rossette asked, once again a pretty, helpless-looking girl on the cusp of becoming a teenager.

'Why, of course, my dear,' Duclos said with a smile. 'Who is prepared to pay the most for a child if it isn't their obscenely rich parents.'

~~~~

In the many years that followed, Duclos and Aline lived happily ever after, as did the other daughters and Rossette, whom Duclos liked to keep a close but distant eye on as she grew. The only child of her apparently totally human, if insanely rich, parents. Rossette lived to be a woman most of the time; the rest of her time seemed to be spent taking a uniquely violent approach to humanitarian relief. Duclos was careful never to provoke the wrath of Rossette, and the two Chimeras never crossed paths again.

Aline spent the rest of her life beside Duclos, becoming her partner in debauchery as she naturally aged whilst Duclos didn't. She never regained the use of the remains of her murderous hand, instead having it amputated, preserved, and displayed in their lavish home. Nevertheless, Aline never did become the twisted and scared old woman she'd, at one point, been desperate to live long enough to become.

Appendix - de Sade's characters mutated into my own

Optional Supporting Information about de Sade's characters above—modernised, mutated, and shaken up

de Sade's Four Libertines/Heroes

The Duc - *is a middle aged, spoilt rich boy who has never grown up and fills his easy life with everything advantage and money can buy. He particularly enjoys the pain of others, especially women and girls. He is prone to extremely violent bouts of temper, both when what he wants is delayed but also for no reason at all except that he is an angry man-child who has gotten away with pulling the wings off flies for far too long.*

Bishop of X - *Duc's slightly younger brother, who was pushed into a high-up position in the church so that he would have a good income whilst the Duc inherited their father's estate. He is a paedophile and sadist who revels in the pain of others, particularly children. However, he is terrified of any potential pain that might be inflicted upon himself. Why didn't he just murder his brother and get the inheritance? Could it be that he likes the Duc, or that, despite being an atheist, he enjoys the high level of power he has as a high-up member of the church? de Sade never answers, although the original book seems to suggest that libertines act only in their own self-interest and that genuine affection for others is a myth.*

President X - *is a repulsive old man who refuses to bathe or practice any personal hygiene whatsoever. He has an unhealthy relationship with alcohol and an unusual fetish for everything and anyone* *normally considered repulsive. He has his fortune and position due to a propensity for committing, organising, and getting away with very nasty murders. He takes particular joy in mutilation and disfigurement.*

Durcet - *A middle aged banker who murdered his family to assure his inheritance. He is a childhood friend of the Duc and a bottom who lives to fulfil his darkest desires with no regard for the suffering it might cause anyone else. Whilst a bottom to his worthy friends, Durcet is a rapist of young men and boys, who suffer greatly for his amusement.*

<u>*The Daughters/ Victims/ Wives of The Libertines*</u>

Constance - *Durcet's daughter who is forced to marry the Duc for the libertine's amusement. She is the eldest of the daughters and, somehow, still remains naturally kind as well as resilient.*

Adelaide - *The President's daughter who is forced to marry Durcet. She is a practising Christian, much to the disgust and mockery of her father and his friends. Despite the danger to herself, she has tried to help her father's victims when possible.*

Julie - *One of the few remaining daughters of the Duc, she is forced to marry the President because her rotten teeth and uncleanliness appeal to him. de Sade presents her as a libertine herself, though of a lesser sort to the men, being merely a woman.*

Aline - *Julie's younger half-sister and the Bishop's daughter. Conceived so that he could have the pleasure of raping his own child. She is the least characterised daughter by de Sade.*

(All are largely beautiful in various ways; all but Julie are described as good, virtuous young women.)

Chimera

The Procuresses/Human Traffickers/Storytellers/Excellent Women who work for rich men, assisting them to shit on others in a more convenient manner.

Duclos – *Middle-aged crime boss who loves making money at any cost. She has both stolen and wasted fortunes—primarily from men like our heroes, whom she flatters and sucks up to whilst secretly holding them in contempt, robbing them blind, and plotting her next move.*

Champville – *Middle-aged pimp, lesbian, and sex toy lover. Will do whatever it takes, with great pleasure, to make her own fortune and get whichever woman she currently desires.*

Martaine – *Middle-aged madam who loves anal. (What can I say? Anal was illegal when de Sade wrote the original.) She is particularly mean-spirited, especially to children, and a dedicated self-preserver who will happily tread on others in order to save herself.*

Desgranges - *Old criminal mastermind and extreme masochist who is missing various body parts, most of her teeth, and is disfigured due to her own pursuits of pleasure and mischief. She is a highly astute criminal, largely for her own dour entrainment. She has a keen brain and is a respected human trafficker and procuress, although she is quickly tiring of sobbing girls and rich degenerates.*

The Duennas- Ugly and old, more minor female criminals

Marie - *Killed her own children rather than raise them. She is a petty thief who has been caught and punished over the years and bears the scars to prove it. She is cruel-natured, particularly to children and animals.*

Louison - *This deviant old hag is very wicked and possesses no sense of right or wrong. She is described as a hunchback who is lame and only has one eye. She has a knack for survival.*
(The libertines plan to make these two capable women governesses to the girls.)

Terese - *Is built like a skeleton who has no hair nor teeth. She also possesses poor hygiene and gum disease, twisted arms, and walks with a limp. She is ruthless and cynical but lives in constant pain. She is a determined woman, but she has been abused constantly since childhood.*

Franchon - *Is an experienced criminal on a similar level to Desgranges. She is motivated by money but is unable to hold on to it and has fallen on hard times. She has a knack for escaping the tricky situations she finds herself in; however, her luck has finally run out. Riddled with cancer and dying, she alleviates the constant pain by being constantly drunk and high. As a result of age and intoxication, she is constantly incontinent and vomiting. By the time she enters the libertines' game, she has developed huge alcohol, drug, and pain tolerances.*

(The libertines plan to make these two women governesses to boys.)

The Harem of Supposedly Physically Perfect Highborn Girls between 12 and 15 who have been kidnapped for the libertines to use and abuse.
Augustine
Fanny
Zelmire
Sophie
Colombe
Hebe
Rosette
Michette

Chimera

The Harem of Supposedly Perfect Highborn Boys between 12 and 15 who have been kidnapped for the libertines to use and abuse.
Zelamir
Cupidon
Narcisse
Zephyr
Adonis
Hyacinthe
Giton

The Fuckers - Men hired by the libertines because of the size of their members and the ability to perform excessively
Hercule
Antinous
Bum-Cleaver
Invictus
(Four other men de Sade doesn't bother naming)

Astrid Addams

Hello, my name is Astrid, and I am a creator. A creator and a creature of many oddities, this story being one of them. My work varies greatly from haunted house fiction to more extreme ideas, to masks to patchwork and appliqué. I am a creature of many contrasting and contradictory personalities and interests hiding behind the placid eyes of a greying thirty-something-year-old. And we all get on great, thank you very much.

As you know by now, my story "Three" was heavily influenced by my reading of the Marquis de Sade's *120 Days of Sodom*. It is a thousand-page-long mostly draft of what would now be classified as extreme horror. Except de Sade wrote it in 1785 over a period of thirty-seven days during the French Revolution. It is a piece of history depicting the attitudes and standards of the time and telling us that extreme horror was within human nature then as it is now. Something has always bothered me about the original text, and that is what I consider to be a massive gap in believability. I cannot believe that the women the brothel keeps—and the old women particularly—would placidly accept the rule of the four spoilt libertines and not take steps to either take their wealth or preserve their own health and lives. A product of the time it was written, perhaps. Then so is my story, for all its references to the original text.

You can find more of my literary creations at:

Amazon – just search Astrid Addams
www.godless.com – just search Astrid Addams

BOBO
Jack Greene

Chimera

WHEN DRAKE NEWPORT entered the diner attached to the truck stop, the other patrons immediately noticed he was different. For some, it was his mottled skin—dark patches like birthmarks all over his pale arms and face. For others, it was the mismatched eyes—one blue and one brown. His hair caught a few eyes too—it was mostly blond but had brown patches in random places in his thick, straggly mane and beard. As he made his way through the quietened diner to an empty seat, the other patrons turned to look away, whispering to one another and hushing curious children.

Drake had been born this way, a fact that had haunted him his whole life. He was used to the stares and whispers and ignored them. He slid into an unoccupied booth at the far end of the diner, his worn jeans adding to the decades of wear and tear of the once cherry-red seats. He took in the scent of coffee and grease and relaxed. He'd been on the road all day and was sick of the scent of diesel and hot tarmac. As he settled in, the noise level in the diner resumed, and people began chatting once more.

As a child, Drake's father had questioned his looks, and a DNA test had eventually been performed. The results were confusing, as Drake's DNA matched neither parent, and had caused many arguments in the household when he was a young child. Eventually, a doctor was able to explain to the warring parents that Drake was a chimera and his looks and DNA anomalies were just a natural genetic hiccup. Although accepting of the explanation, the damage was already done, and Drake's father never saw his son as his own.

'Can I get you some coffee to start you off?' a young waitress asked him, her brunette hair tied in a ponytail and her makeup fresh and bright.

'Sure thing,' Drake said, and the waitress, whose nametag read Delilah, began to fill a white mug with the dark liquid from the glass jug in her hand.

'Thank you kindly,' Drake drawled gently at her, and she smiled and walked away.

Drake took in the scent of the coffee before adding sugar and creamer from the dispensers on the table. He took a few sips and let the delicious caffeine take a hold of his senses. Once he was feeling a little better, he took a laminated menu from the tidy table and glanced over it. He'd been here plenty of times, but he always liked to read the menu in case they'd added something new. The waitress was definitely new; that was for sure. Drake idly gazed around the brightly lit diner to see if he could spot who she'd replaced.

Behind the pristine white counter were Susie and Ann-Margaret, as usual. Both women were older, salt of the earth types, no-nonsense women who would treat you right as long as you were polite. Drake was always polite. He couldn't see Sandy, though, and that wasn't a surprise, as he remembered she would drop things a lot and was nervous around men. *Not gonna last long in a place like this,* Drake thought to himself.

'Are you ready to order, sir?' Delilah asked, smiling, back at his table with a little pad of paper and a small pencil at the ready.

'I'll take the hamburger and fries, no onions, and a slice of blueberry pie for dessert,' Drake said.

'Would you like cream or ice cream on your pie?' Delilah asked.

'Cream, please,' Drake replied, and she thanked him with a nod and walked away.

Drake used the restroom, and when he returned to his booth, his coffee had been refilled. He looked around the room, again noticing the furtive glances and whispering that always accompanied him in public. He didn't look normal enough, and it always put him on edge. As he took in the various folk—some truckers like himself, a couple of families with kids who were staring, the odd lone traveller—he noticed someone at the counter that looked familiar.

The man had scruffy dark hair, a beard with grey flecks in it, and wore the usual trucker garb. He had piercing blue eyes, which Drake noticed in the mirror behind the counter. This man looked just like his dad had looked back when …

NO! I mustn't think about that! Drake fought the memory, as he always did. The memory came anyway, as it always did.

Drake was 10 years old again, back in his momma's kitchen in their tiny apartment. The cupboards were a faded green, and the floor was white and tiled. His parents were arguing, as they did most days. The sound of a screaming baby in another room added to the cacophony. Mom hadn't made Dad the right dinner, and Dad had thrown the food on the floor, which Mom was trying to clean up while crying. There was spaghetti and sauce everywhere, and Drake remembered reaching out for a handful, as he was hungry; he hadn't eaten all day. Seeing this, his dad exploded and slapped the child's hand, making him drop the food. The pain stung his small hand, and he yelped in shock. Then the beating began.

The blows seemed endless, each one a fresh pain as fists and then feet connected with his young skin. Drake felt every blow as if he were there, reliving the agony over and over again. The boy finally curled up into a ball, screaming for his father to stop, wanting to be anywhere but there. Why was his dad doing this to him? What had he done? He felt so alone and afraid. Mom stood up for him then; her first act of bravery, and her last. She pushed Dad away, screaming at him to leave the boy alone. What happened next stayed with Drake forever.

Dad began punching Drake's mom repeatedly in the face, breaking her nose with the first blow, and blood came streaming out immediately. Drake watched through fingers clutched tightly over his face as his mom hit the ground with a sickening thud. Dad kept punching Mom, and now her blood was spattering the walls, the floor, the cupboards, and Drake's small body. Drake could still hear the awful wet sound as each blow caused her to bleed more and resist less. Dad grew tired of using his fists and started kicking Mom. Her screams had died down to whimpering once she'd fallen to the floor, and now she was barely making any sound at all. When she stopped moving or making any sound save for the guttural rasping of her ragged breath, Dad pulled the hunting knife from his belt and stabbed her over and over again. The stench of iron and sweat was seared into Drake's memory as he recalled blow after blow slashing the pale skin. He could see bone, muscle, blood, everything as his father kept stabbing until he ran out of energy. He

84

then turned and left, cleaning the knife blade on the kitchen curtains as he did so.

Drake lay on the ground, beyond tears and horror, as he looked into his dead mother's lifeless blue eyes in her mangled face. Her cheekbone protruded through her flattened nose, her blond hair was tinged with red, and there were chunks of something from her broken jaw on her neck. He hardly recognised what was left of her, but those blue eyes, he would never forget.

'Would you like ketchup, sir?' a voice said, pulling him back to the present.

'No, thank you,' Drake said, inwardly shuddering at the thought of the red sauce.

'Enjoy your meal,' Delilah said and smiled at him.

'I'm sure I will,' Drake replied and gave her a smile.

As he ate, Drake watched the man at the counter as he also ordered food and ate it. Drake was ahead of him timewise, so he ate leisurely while he formulated his plan. The guy had a deep tan on his left arm, which meant he was probably going north. He'd be on the far side of the truck stop if he'd entered from the south entrance, and that meant he wasn't too far from Drake's own truck. He was new to this stop, as he'd just sassed Ann-Margaret and she'd ignored his requests for a top up of coffee. Nobody sassed the waitresses twice. He recognised a few regulars and narrowed down the possible truck the man drove from what he could see from his booth by the window. It was going to be easy, Drake thought.

□□□□

FBI agents Kevin Langley and Stephanie Sparrow had arrived at their destination after a tiring flight and drive from Quantico. Langley was in his mid-40s, a little dishevelled from the flight, and was currently glaring at his partner as she told him once again to shave his beard off. Sparrow was almost two decades his junior, and he was not about to let a rookie tell him what to do. He glared at the young woman with her long, curly blond hair and ridiculous smart attire. They were in the middle of a truck stop, and she was practically wearing a neon sign on her head that said FBI. He, on the other hand, had the good sense to dress for the part. A checked shirt, jeans, and a scruffy beard were part of the uniform here. He ignored her and walked towards the diner to scope it out.

'Go check the trucks to see if our perp is here,' Langley said to Sparrow when she began to follow him to the diner.

'But—' she began, ready to cite some regulation or other.

'I'm the senior agent here; go check the damn trucks!' he barked at her.

Stephanie stopped in her tracks and sighed.

'Fine!' she said. 'But remember what we discussed on the plane.'

'Yeah, yeah,' Langley said as he walked away from her.

Sparrow turned and walked over to where the trucks were parked while the drivers were eating, showering, or sleeping. Her smart shoes, though flats, rang out on the tarmac as she walked. The scent of diesel fuel permeated everything, and she wondered if she'd ever get the smell out of her black pantsuit. A few men were walking about here and there. One woman, rather large and with bigger muscles than most of the men, nodded at her and winked as she passed. This unnerved Sparrow more, and she had to take a deep breath and remember her training as she continued to the parked trucks.

'Our unsub is likely a trucker, preying on transients and other truckers as he travels the interstates across the country,' Sparrow had reminded Langley whilst still on the plane.

'I know,' Langley had replied, sniffing the remnants of the shot glass in his hand.

'My point is that you fit the profile of his victims, and you should change your attire accordingly,' Sparrow said, glaring at the older agent from her window seat.

'I can handle myself,' Langley said. 'Having my beard this long will help me blend in and make it easier to talk to the other truckers.'

'I'm just saying,' Sparrow replied with a gentle sigh, 'don't blame me if you find yourself dead at the side of the road with your penis chopped off.'

'Not gonna happen,' Langley replied, and then tipped the last remnants of his whisky into his mouth.

Sparrow had glanced through the photos of victims as Langley ordered another whisky, the gore and violence still shocking no matter how many times she viewed the pictures. The bodies were all Caucasian men, bearded and aged between 25 and 60. They were all beaten profusely, the face the main target, which indicated a rage-induced motive. This person was going after a type, one that reminded him of someone from his life who had caused him harm somehow. The final act was to remove the penis; none of the missing members had ever been recovered. Sparrow hoped they would not be finding a trophy room somewhere filled with the remnants. The bodies were always left at the side of an interstate, usually hidden by bushes, although the last few had been left more in the open.

Now, Stephanie wondered if she was going to be the one dead at the side of the interstate. She pulled herself together mentally and continued on towards the trucks parked further ahead. They were looking for a dark blue or black truck with a large dent in the passenger side front fender. The description had been given to them by a reliable witness and corroborated by CCTV footage, albeit grainy. They could not make out the truck's licence plate in the video, but the dent was plainly visible. The truck had been headed in this direction, according to the witness, and this was the most logical truck stop to refuel at. Sparrow just had to find the truck, if it was here, before the driver returned to it.

It was dark, which meant identifying truck colours was trickier, but Sparrow could quickly dismiss any pale trucks at once. From a quick visual glance, there were six dark trucks that could be the one they were looking for, and Sparrow started walking towards the nearest one to check for damage. The first four were undamaged in that area, but number five was a possibility. Sparrow checked the grainy pictures from the camera again, which she had stored on her phone, and matched the damaged area with the truck in front of her. It seemed to be a match. Just to eliminate the last truck, Sparrow quickly walked down a hundred yards to the last truck to check it. Once she had eliminated the dark-green older truck, she returned to the one she suspected.

This dark blue truck was fairly dirty but in good condition apart from the dent. The doors on either side and the trailer door at the rear were spotless, though, which raised Sparrow's suspicions. Possible clean up after a murder? She thought so. Sparrow took a picture of the truck's licence plate with her phone camera and sent it to FBI HQ to see if there were any priors on the truck and to find out who the driver was.

□ □ □ □

Langley entered the diner and found a seat at the counter, squeezing his aching overweight buttocks onto the well-worn bar stool. It wasn't comfortable, and he immediately looked around at his fellow diners to see how they managed to sit like this for long. To his left was a blond-haired trucker with blue eyes. Looked to be about the same age as Langley. He glanced at the man's posture, and he seemed comfortable and at ease. Maybe sitting in a truck for hours every day made bar stools a better seat option, Langley wondered. The woman to his right was dressed in a dark red dress, very tight and short, with black stockings and high heels. Her stocking tops peeked out from under her short hem, and she was wearing a lacy black bra that made itself apparent from her low-cut top. She was obviously here looking for clients, Langley thought to himself. She made stool-sitting into an art form, her legs crossed and posture upright, looking comfortable and alluring.

While he waited for someone to offer him coffee, Langley stared in the mirror behind the coffee machine and tried to get a good look at the other patrons in the diner. From his position, he could make out a couple of families in booths, a young man in jeans and button-down shirt flirting with one of the waitresses, and a trucker eating a burger. He couldn't make out any details about most of the diners, as they either had their backs to him or other furniture and people were in the way.

He decided to choose a better table and slid off the stool carefully. Glancing around, Langley spotted a small table in the far corner and settled in there instead. His back and buttocks immediately thanked him for this welcome relief.

Now he had a better view, Langley looked around the diner to take in the other patrons properly. He dismissed anyone travelling with a companion, any women, and the young man in the shirt, as he was too young to have a trucker's licence. That left three possibilities. The blue-eyed man at the counter, the blond-haired man with the burger, or the third man who had just walked in. This new arrival was wearing clean, new clothing and was freshly showered. He carried a black case that could have been for a guitar, and all the waitresses glanced over at him, smiling. Langley immediately dismissed this newcomer, as he was not a trucker. No, it had to be Blondie or Blue-Eyes, as he'd designated them.

'Coffee?' a woman asked, blocking his view of the rest of the diner abruptly.

'Sure, thank you,' Langley replied and smiled at her.

'Here you go,' she replied, pouring coffee from her glass jug into a waiting mug on the table.

'Thanks,' Langley said, and the woman bustled off to other tables.

Langley sipped the coffee immediately, without adding sugar or creamer. He looked around the diner again and noticed Blondie had disappeared. The burger had been eaten and the fries consumed. There was an additional plate with a purple residue, probably pie, which was also on the table. A pile of money was tucked under this plate, indicating the food was finished and the man on his way. Langley had to make a quick decision: follow Blondie or stay on Blue-Eyes. Looking over at the trucker at the counter, Langley realised he was still eating his sandwich and had a plate of pie and cream still to eat. He could nip out and check where Blondie had gone while Blue-Eyes was still eating. Leaving the rest of his coffee untouched, Langley left the diner and headed out into the night.

Drake didn't head to his truck right away; instead, he scoped out the other trucks to see if he could clearly identify the truck his 'dad' was driving. *No, not Dad*, Drake reminded himself; Dad was in prison. He paused as he felt screaming in his head and tried to breathe deeply to regain control. He smelt blood and saw flesh in his mind, and the screaming became louder. He could never tell if it was his screaming, his mother's screaming, or the screams of his baby sister. He tried not to think about her either. Sally-Jaye would probably be an adult by now, but he wouldn't know her if she walked up to him and said hello. Foster families were happy to take cute little girls but not traumatised ten-year-old boys. He'd never seen her after she was taken to the foster home when she was three.

91

Drake shook his head to clear his thoughts and continued on to the white truck that he'd pinpointed as the new guy's truck.

The truck and trailer were very new, Drake realised. There were the usual dirt marks from the road, but other than that, it could have been driven out of the factory last week. The cab was clean and tidy, there was almost no trash, and he could see a small suitcase on the passenger seat. This trucker was as green as they came, Drake thought. Perfect. This one would make the screaming stop easily. With his recon completed, Drake headed to his truck to prepare things for his guest.

□□□□

Sparrow had been watching the truck for ten minutes when someone walked up to it and opened the trailer at the back. Luckily, she was hidden behind a dumpster with a badly drawn squirrel on it and was crouched down in the shadows. She had just received some information from HQ on the truck and its driver, and she carefully reviewed this on her phone, with the brightness turned down and shielding the glare with her left hand. The truck belonged to Drake Newport, a trucker of eight years. His driver's licence photo was somewhat grainy, but she could make out a few features. There were no violations, and he had never so much as received a speeding ticket. There were no criminal charges, although he had a sealed juvenile record that she couldn't access as of yet. She'd already forwarded a request for the records to be unsealed, but that might take days. Still, from what info she had, he didn't seem like a serial killer to Sparrow.

◻◻◻◻

Langley followed Blondie as he checked out the white truck, intrigued as to what he was doing. Once the man had given the truck a once over, he'd left to go to a different truck, and Langley dismissed it as curiosity or envy. A brand-new truck was going to get some looks, he assumed. As Langley carefully followed Blondie, he received a text message from his partner. He stopped and took a few steps back behind a red truck to check the message. Luckily, his phone was on vibrate, as was standard procedure, so it didn't alert Blondie to his presence.

Found the truck, driver clean besides juvie records.

A photo of the licence plate was sent, as well as the driver's details, including driver's licence information. It was Blondie all right, Langley realised, looking at the driver's licence photo. He enlarged the picture on his phone screen and studied the picture carefully. He realised the guy had one blue eye and one brown. His hair was also patchy, something he hadn't realised when following the man, as he was wearing a baseball cap.

Eyes are different colours, could explain the differing descriptions, Sparrow texted next.

'Yeah, no shit,' Langley muttered under his breath.

He resumed following Blondie, or Drake, using his real name, and wasn't surprised to spot Sparrow hiding in the shadows nearby. Drake had entered the rear of the trailer and closed the doors, so they had a few minutes to discuss what to do next. Langley slid behind the dumpster next to Sparrow and hunkered down next to her, his knees complaining with a series of clicks and clunks. Langley grimaced and then spoke quietly to his partner.

'He was scoping out the white truck,' Langley whispered.

'The new one?' Sparrow asked.

'Yeah, I thought he might just be envious of it at first, but I dunno.'

'Seems a bit suspicious if you ask me. Normally, if someone wants to look at a vehicle, they ask the driver for a good look, not creep about at night while the driver is gone,' Sparrow replied.

'There's another trucker at the diner I thought fit the description of our unsub,' Langley said.

'Did he look fairly clean and young?' Sparrow asked.

'No, not clean, bearded and straggly hair, blue eyes. Both guys looked like they could fit the description. This one left first, though. Interesting how he's the driver of the truck we're looking for, though.'

'Do you think he's setting up a kill room in the trailer?' Sparrow asked.

'Possibly,' Langley replied, noticing the hint of excitement in her voice.

'Maybe we should go in now and catch him in the act?' Sparrow asked, her eyes wide with possibilities.

'No, Sparrow,' Langley reprimanded her. 'Remember your training. We need just cause to enter the truck, and we might ruin the case if he's just minding his own business in there. We have to wait until he takes a victim.'

'What if the victim is already in the trailer?' Sparrow asked.

'He's not. Remember he was checking out the white truck. Probably going to take the driver of that truck and then kill him. Probably the blue eyes fellow. We need to watch and wait. I know this is your first serial killer case, Sparrow, so take a deep breath and remember protocol,' Langley said.

'Yes, yes, of course,' Sparrow replied, annoyed at herself for getting carried away.

□ □ □ □

Drake set up the trailer for the kill. There was plenty of room inside, as the goods he was transporting were tucked in and tied at the far end on plastic-wrapped pallets, leaving a good ten feet of usable area. He laid out a few tarps he kept for the occasion and brushed them out flat. These he washed each time, but they had some stains and tears from age. Drake made a mental note to destroy them and buy more next time. Then he checked his hunting knife, making sure it was clean and sharp. Once he was satisfied all was ready, he left the trailer and walked round to the front of the truck.

'Hey, Blue!' Drake said as he opened the front driver's side door.

A large dark-furred dog barked excitedly, wagging a bushy tail as Drake opened the door. The dog had one blue eye and one brown, much like its owner, one of the reasons Drake took the dog in to begin with. The other was its appetite for certain human remains. Drake snapped a leash on the dog's collar, and he took it for a walk to do its business. Blue spent some time walking around, sniffing at the trucks, and then found a tree to mark with its scent.

After that, it sniffed about a little more, getting closer to a dumpster that was covered in a child's drawings of squirrels. Then Blue turned around and decided this was the spot to poop. Drake waited for the dog to finish and then scooped it up with a plastic bag from his pocket. This he deposited in the dumpster nearby, not noticing the two people crouched low and quiet beyond.

Drake then walked his dog around the truck stop, glancing around at the diner every minute or so, waiting for his prey to emerge. Presently, the trucker that resembled his father appeared, but instead of going to his truck, the man walked over to the shower block, a bag over one shoulder. He was obviously going to be a while in there, showering and getting changed. Drake decided to take Blue back to the truck and go with plan B instead. Having a dog as a distraction was good, but grabbing the guy in the shower worked just as well for him.

☐☐☐☐

Langley and Sparrow were practiced in keeping still and quiet, but even so, it was pretty nerve-wracking to have their quarry in such close proximity. When he'd moved on with the dog, Sparrow released a careful, quiet breath of relief and tried to relax and get her racing heart under control. Once Drake was around the corner and out of sight, the two agents stood up and moved away from the dumpster. Langley's back and knees were sore, and he spent a few moments stretching out his aching muscles. Sparrow kept a close eye on where their suspect was going next. They watched as he walked aimlessly about with the dog, noticing his furtive glances at the diner. When he spotted the other trucker leaving the diner and returned the dog to the truck, they knew what he was going to do next.

☐☐☐☐

Drake made for the shower block, keeping his pace slow and easy, and looking about for witnesses as he did so. He'd been eyeballed a couple of times in the past, but so far, he'd managed to get away with it. He wanted that to continue. He approached the door to the shower block and looked casually behind him as he reached for the door handle. A few folks were moving about, but none were looking his way, and they all seemed to have their own business to attend to. He entered the building and closed the door quietly behind him.

The room was tiled floor to ceiling in cracked and aging white tiles. There were several toilet cubicles on the right-hand side and four shower cubicles on the left. At the end of the room were several sinks and hand driers. The toilet doors were all ajar, and a quick glance under the partitions confirmed the cubicles were indeed empty. There was only one shower in use; the other three doors were open and empty, and the far shower stall was the only one occupied. Dad had to be in there, Drake thought.

No! Not Dad!

The sound of the shower brought back a memory of long ago. Dad in the shower, getting clean after a long day's work, the smell of the lemon-scented soap clear in his mind. Mom was somewhere in the apartment with Sally-Jaye, and Drake was alone in the single bedroom their home had. There was a double bed, a

97

cot, and a small blow-up mattress on the floor where Drake slept. Blankets were strewn over it, and Drake sat amongst them, dreading what was coming next. Daddy came home from work, had his shower, and then it was THAT time before dinner.

'Boy! Get in here and scrub your daddy's back!'

Terrified, Drake contemplated not going in there and instead running away and never coming back. But Dad always found him, and then there'd be a beating on top of the other thing. He felt his heart pick up speed and the fear inside him grow. On legs seemingly made of rubber, Drake stood and walked towards the bathroom.

'You'd better get in here now!' the angry voice commanded.

As if he were a zombie, Drake's body obeyed the summons and entered the bathroom. He fumbled at his clothing, removing the well-worn jeans and t-shirt, dropping them to the floor. Once his underwear was also off, Drake stepped into the shower with his dad and reached for the sponge.

'What you looking at?' a voice shouted, pulling Drake out of his memory sharply.

'Uh, sorry, I'm new here. Is this the shower block?' Drake asked.

'Yeah, it sure is,' the blue-eyed man replied, and sat at a nearby bench to dry off.

He was wrapped in a clean white towel, his light-brown hair wet and curly, and his beard fresh and clean. His vivid blue eyes turned away from Drake after watching him for a moment too long, and then he concentrated on getting dry and dressed.

Drake sat down on the other end of the wooden bench and then realised he didn't have a towel with him. He felt stupid at his obvious mistake and went to stand up again and leave the shower block.

'You're not really here for a shower, are you?' the man asked, smiling coyly at Drake.

'Uh, no,' Drake replied, caught off guard. 'How could you tell?'

'No towel, no clean clothes,' the man replied.

'Yeah, I er—' Drake began, but the other man cut him off.

'I saw you looking at me in the diner earlier,' he said.

'You did?' Drake asked.

'Yes, I saw how your eyes wandered over my body; I saw it in the mirror,' he said and grinned.

'Oh,' Drake said, suddenly realising what he was implying. 'I didn't realise. I didn't know if you were into guys.'

'Guys, gals, whoever, really,' he replied and winked at Drake. 'I'm Bryan, by the way, Bryan with a Y.'

'Hey, Bryan, I'm Drake.'

'Do you want to fuck here or in my truck?' Bryan asked, catching Drake off guard again.

'Oh, er, well, not here, they'll ban us from the truck stop if we get caught.' Drake had seen that happen before.

'My place or yours?' Bryan asked, accidentally dropping his towel to the floor.

'Mine?' Drake asked, wondering how he'd lucked out on getting his prey back to his truck so easily.

'Fabulous,' Bryan said and began to get dressed, slowly and seductively.

~~~~

'You should go in there,' Sparrow hissed at Langley.

'No, we wait. The kill is never in the showers; it's not his MO,' Langley replied.

'As far as we know,' Sparrow replied, glaring at her obstinate partner.

'Trust me, there's no killing going on in there,' Langley replied.

'Fine!' Sparrow said, crossing her arms defiantly. 'But if the victim dies, it's on your head.'

'Fine,' Langley replied and crossed his arms mockingly.

They were standing at the pumps, trying to look like customers and blend in with the people around them. The smell of diesel and gas mingled in Sparrow's nose and made her feel a little nauseous. She felt a little out of place amongst the rough and ready truckers and long-distance travellers refuelling here, with her smart attire. Maybe Langley was right after all, she thought bitterly. Something about the attire that truckers wore, though, it just made her feel uncomfortable, and she didn't know why. Smart was her thing, and she felt at her best when wearing it. A few moments later, Drake and the other trucker emerged from the shower block together, walking side by side. As they walked slowly to Drake's blue truck, Sparrow glanced at Langley to be rewarded with a smug 'I told you so' look on his face.

The agents waited for the pair of truckers to make their way towards the truck before following at a discreet distance. Knowing the destination helped, and they skirted around cars and trucks to remain unseen. When they arrived at the blue truck with the dent, Sparrow couldn't see where the pair had gone for a moment.

Langley crept up to the cab, gesturing for Sparrow to stay behind and cover his rear. He peered in through the cab window and was greeted by Blue, barking at him from the otherwise empty cab. Langley backed away quickly, and Blue settled down, his job done for now. The two agents retreated behind the next truck and waited for a few minutes to see if the dog's barking had alerted the suspect. When there was no movement in their direction, Langley gestured to Sparrow that they should approach the rear of the trailer, and then he unholstered his gun.

Sparrow listened at the door of the trailer for a few moments but could not hear anything going on inside. She then pulled her gun and covered Langley as he reached for the handle to the trailer door. It was large and unwieldy, but he managed to flip it open and swing the huge door back and aside. Sparrow pointed her gun at the inside of the trailer and waited for Langley to give the word to enter. It was dimly lit inside, with pallets of goods to the far end. At this end, several tarps were laid out on the floor, and a portable lamp shone from one side, lighting up the scene in the middle of the tarps.

Bryan lay naked on the tarp, his face bloody and bruised, his eyes closed. It was hard to tell if he was unconscious or already dead at that point in time. Drake sat astride the man with a large knife held in both hands, a manic look on his face. He was also naked, and the full extent of his skin patterning was evident. Patches of pale and dark skin mosaicked his torso and legs, his one blue eye gleaming in the light while the brown one seemed blacker than hell. And at that moment, he looked as if he were two people fused into one. He froze when the doors were opened and was now uncertain what to do next.

Sparrow stared at Drake's blood-spattered face, the mismatched eyes and blond hair suddenly calling up a memory long forgotten.

She was small again and in a place that was strange yet somehow familiar to her. She'd heard screaming a while ago, and now silence, and she had gone to see what was going on. She was hungry and scared. In front of her, as she walked around the corner of a room, she saw a boy lying on the floor, curled up and sobbing. He was covered in blood, his blond straggly hair covering part of his face but his eyes clearly visible—one blue and one brown. Next to him was an unrecognisable shape on the floor. It was a mess of red and pink with long yellow strands here and there. It looked a bit like spaghetti to the little girl. She reached out to the boy on the ground, her brother, and prodded him on the shoulder repeatedly.

'Bobo?' Sparrow spoke aloud.

'Sally-Jaye?' Drake replied, staring incredulously at the FBI agent.

'Bobo,' she said again, trying the name out for the first time in over 20 years. 'Are you Bobo?'

'Bobo is what my baby sister called me coz she couldn't say brother,' Drake replied. 'But I haven't seen her in a long time. You can't be her.'

'I remember a brother lying on the ground, covered in blood, and a big pile of spaghetti nearby,' Sparrow replied, trying to make sense of the patchy memory that had just appeared.

'That wasn't spaghetti; that was what was left of my mom after Daddy killed her,' Drake replied.

'I don't remember any of that,' Sparrow said, her hands falling slowly to her sides.

'I do,' Drake replied. 'I never could forget.'

'I know I was adopted at about three years old and that my parents had died, but they never told me I had a brother,' Sparrow said.

'Oh, he ain't dead. He's still in prison rotting away for the murders he did,' Drake said.

'He's alive?' Sparrow asked, feeling a spike of anger she had never felt before.

'Yup,' Drake replied bitterly, 'living an easy life behind bars with three squares a day and a comfy bed to sleep in at night. Bastard.'

'I can't believe it, after all these years. I thought I was alone, but I have a brother.' Sparrow could feel tears welling up in her eyes, and she almost forgot her partner just a few feet away from her for a moment.

Langley, however, had not forgotten where he was and who he was with.

~~~~

'I hate to break up this family reunion, but you're under arrest. Drop the knife, climb off the dead body, and lie face down on the floor.' Langley waved the end of his handgun to indicate the direction Drake should move in.

Drake looked from one agent to the other. The older man looked sturdy and knew his way around the gun. There was no way he could overpower him before getting shot. Sally-Jaye, if it was her, would be easy to rush, but again, the man would shoot him. He dropped the knife on Bryan's naked chest and raised his hands, looking about for any way out of this situation. His biggest fear was being put in jail with his father. As he awkwardly clambered off the dead body, arms raised and slipping in the pools of blood, Drake spotted a small revolver poking out of the back pocket of Bryan's jeans, which were discarded nearby. If he could just reach that, he could shoot his way out of the trailer, set Blue loose, and in the chaos, head for the dead man's truck.

'I gotta ask,' Langley said, and Drake's head shot up as the FBI agent spoke. 'What did you do with all the private parts?'

'Well, if you must know,' Drake said, waiting for the split second when the agent would gag from the response to grab the weapon, 'I fed them to my dog.'

Agent Langley blinked; for a moment, the image of a dog eating the genitals of dead men flickering in his mind's eye. That was when Drake lunged for the gun, sliding in the sticky red mess on the floor of the trailer and managing to grasp it just in time. He raised the gun and pointed it at the senior FBI agent and slid the safety off. Langley stared at Drake, and Drake stared back at Langley. Both men had a gun pointed at the other, and both had the hard gaze of someone who was about to pull the trigger.

Sparrow watched the scene calmly, the tears that had welled up before now gone, replaced with the need to break this stalemate. On her left, a long-lost brother she never knew she had until now;

on her right, the stubborn, old-fashioned partner who never seemed to listen to her. Stephanie Sparrow raised her gun, chose her side, and fired her weapon. Discharging a firearm inside a small metal container made her immediately deaf, albeit temporarily. Her ears screamed a high-pitched note while the metallic scent of musky gunpowder filled her nostrils. The muzzle flash also temporarily blinded her somewhat, making her view from the end of the barrel blurred.

'Oh God, no!' Sparrow shouted as she looked at the sprawled figure on the ground, 'What have I done?'

She knew she would regret her decision for the rest of her life.

Jack Greene

Jack has been writing horror and sci-fi for many years now, and has been self-publishing for quite a few of those. This story was inspired by the biological definition of chimera mixed in with Jack's fascination for serial killers and the workings of the human mind. Other stories Jack has written include Vermin, Osmosis, Silver Blood and Empty Devils, with many more in the pipeline to come. This is the first inclusion in an anthology, and hopefully, there will be more in the future.

TRINITY
DE McCluskey

1.

'SIR, HE'S AWAKE.'

The voice was stoic in its report. There was not an ounce of emotion in it. Colonel Lewis looked up from his desk at the young man addressing him. *He's going to go far in his career,* he thought randomly. He nodded at the private and stood.

His bones creaked as he rose from the chair, and there was a shot of pain in both knees. Even though he didn't quite look it—or, for that matter, act it—today, he was feeling every single day of his fifty-seven years. He bit the inside of his lip. 'How is he?' He regretted the question the instant it left his mouth. This soldier wouldn't know how he was. All he'd know was the poor bastard was alive, and that would be the end of it for him.

The soldier shrugged. 'He's awake,' he replied.

Lewis grabbed his jacket, a packet of cigarettes, and pointed to the door of his office. 'Let's go, then.'

As they marched through the barracks, young men of indeterminable age but all looking the same—fit, healthy fighting machines with cropped hair and immaculate uniforms—stopped what they were doing and stood to attention, saluting the Colonel as he passed. He nodded to every single one of them. In times like this, the men needed to know there was a chain of command. No matter how rough it got, you could still look to your superior officers.

No matter what happens to our boys, Lewis thought, *Uncle Sam is still looking out for them.*

'Fucking Russians,' he mumbled under his breath as he strode confidently through the barracks, heading towards the hospital wing.

'What was that, sir?' the private escorting him asked, looking back over his shoulder.

Lewis shook his head. 'Nothing, Private, carry on.'

The soldier knocked on the door and announced the Colonel. Everyone snapped to attention as if he were a three-star general. 'As you were,' he replied to the attention, and everyone in the room visibly relaxed. He wasn't a fan of the pomp and circumstance of his rank in this unit.

He knew that now *he* was awake, others would come and take over. He had no problem with this. In fact, he welcomed it. He wanted to distance himself from this circus. This situation could have pretty dire consequences for the so-called Cold War being fought between the USA and the USSR. Ever since the end of WWII, when the human race had temporarily stopped looking at each other with suspicious eyes and started looking greedily and suspiciously to the stars, the USA and the USSR, once allies against the Nazis, found themselves in a situation where they just couldn't trust each other.

The space race, on both sides, even though widely acknowledged, was officially *secret.*

For some reason, everyone wanted to get to the moon all of a sudden.

Lewis didn't know why. He'd once been an ace pilot. He'd even shot down a few Krauts during *double-u, double-u, aye, aye,* but he had absolutely no desire to travel beyond the world he had fought so hard for, and he couldn't understand why anyone else would.

'Is the patient in any condition to talk?' he asked the doctor who was coming out of a small room. The words RESTRICTED ACCESS were plastered over the window. The doctor was only a young man. Lewis thought he couldn't be much of a doctor if he was below forty, but he was the best they had been given, and he *did seem* to be pretty good at his job.

'He is, sir. Listen, there's something you should know before going in there.'

Colonel Lewis stopped him. 'I don't have time to be briefed, Doctor. This is a matter of national security, and I need to get in there, even if that means going in cold.'

'OK, but you understand we can't have him being exposed to high levels of stress and anxiety, don't you?'

'I promise you, Doc. I'll be in and out. All I want to do is get him well enough to talk a little. I need to know what those Russkies did to him.'

The doctor smiled a humourless smile. 'Well, without giving too much away, they did a number on him, all right. We've taken scans and bloods, and we're looking into all of that now, just to make sure there's nothing untoward, but he's awake, although weak and drowsy right now.'

'Is he lucid?'

'As lucid as he's been since ...'

The doctor left his sentence hanging. The colonel nodded, understanding what was *not* said, and entered the room. The curtains were drawn, and the lights were dim. The space was filled with machines that were bleeping and pinging and casting green glows into the darkened room, giving it an eerie feeling. There was no one else inside other than him, the doctor, and the man in the bed, who was covered in bandages.

The patient was deep in the shadows as he lay on top of the blankets. The bandages were wrapped tightly around the top of his head, his face, and the lower parts of his arms. He was wearing long pyjama bottoms, and his feet were covered in socks. The white vest covering his mostly bandaged torso was pristine.

'Captain Furtado,' the colonel addressed him as he entered the room.

The patient's head turned just a little, but he offered no further acknowledgement of Lewis's rank, or indeed his presence.

'It's about time we had a little chat. The good doctor here tells me you're in good enough shape to talk.'

The figure nodded, only slightly. He lifted his arm and gestured towards the seat next to the bed. 'Colonel, please sit.'

Goosebumps rose on Lewis's arms. There was something about his voice, something that was just not right. The patient had gone through something terrible, possibly indescribable, and Lewis could understand how something like that could take it out of a man physically ...

But *that* voice!

The colonel took the offered seat. His eyes gestured towards the doctor, who took the hint and left the room. 'I'll be outside if you need me.' He glanced back, just once, at the patient and left quicker than the colonel thought necessary.

'So, Captain. We, and when I say we, I mean the military, need to know what happened to you up there. Why you were the only one to return from the mission, and why the Russians did what they did to your ship.'

The patient sighed. There was a wet, warbling sound as the air expelled from his lungs. The colonel was reminded of water sluicing from a drainpipe. Another shudder tore through him, but he made pains not to show it.

'The first thing you need to know, Colonel, is that space … it's *big!*'

2.

'CAPTAIN FURTADO, YOU'RE clear for launch.'

They were the words the three men had been waiting to hear for the last two hours. They'd been sat on the launchpad waiting for clearance for what felt like weeks. All the systems had been checked and double checked. The propulsion rockets were functioning, their air tanks were full, and they were raring to go.

Five traumatic and exhilarating minutes later, they were in orbit, roughly twenty thousand kilometres above sea level.

The three-man module was up, the separation from the propulsion tanks, normally the trickiest part of take-off, had gone smoothly, and the small craft was speeding around the planet. Furtado looked at his pilot, Green, with a grin. He offered a thumbs-up. The gesture was then passed on by Green to Engineer Mallon to his left.

'We've done it, boys,' Furtado said through the coms in their helmets. 'We're officially the first Americans to reach a stable orbit. Fuck those Russkies and their dog, eh?' he laughed.

'All systems normal, Captain,' Green reported, looking at the dials before him.

'We have a slight mis-pressure on the starboard thrust, but I can align it. Other than that, the old Hermes IV is in good shape,' Mallon offered.

'Excellent. Let's spin this thing and get ourselves home for dinner. What do you say, men? Cocktails at my pl—'

A screaming alarm interrupted the celebrations. It pulsed at a high pitch, cutting through the roar of the engines, straight into the consciousness of all three men.

'What's that?' Furtado snapped.

Mallon bashed away at the keypad on his console. He regarded the screens accessible to him. He shook his head.

'What?' Furtado snapped again.

'It's a proximity alarm.'

'A proximity alarm? That was only installed as a precaution. There can't be anything out there in our proximity.'

'The alarm would beg to differ, sir,' Mallon offered, still looking in his monitors. 'All I can see is darkness. I can't see any stars or get a location on Earth.'

'Check again. Believe me, Earth is still there. Can you get a reading on the moon?'

Mallon shook his head. 'Nothing, sir. It's just darkness out there.'

'Not *just* darkness,' Green chipped in. His hands were gripping the controls of the module as if life itself depended on them. 'Look ...'

3.

'WHY DO YOU need to know, Colonel?' The voice was cold and raspy, difficult to read. Lewis didn't know if the man was being defiant, or if he was genuinely interested in why the Pentagon was so interested in him.

'National—'

The laugh that came from the patient made his skin crawl. His legs suddenly felt like jelly.

'Please don't give me any of that national security bullshit, Colonel. We're both better than that,' the wet voice hissed.

Lewis had been briefed that the patient could be snappy, quick to anger, but after everything he'd been through, everything he'd witnessed, they were to give him an allowance.

'I was going to say, national heroes are always in the thoughts of the Pentagon.'

Furtado grunted; it sounded like half laugh, half admonishment. 'I was in space for less than five minutes.'

'You were gone for three years, Peter.'

Furtado fell silent as if he were contemplating the time he was away for. 'Three years?' he asked, his strange voice changing—

it now sounded distant. 'That can't be. We only just got to orbit. Mallon was navigating, and Green was—'

'Watching the monitors for collisions.' It was Lewis's turn to finish for him.

'That's right. We were celebrating a perfect launch, when from out of nowhere ...'

4.

HE WASN'T ALONE. There was movement around him. He couldn't see anything, only sense it. He couldn't hear much of anything either, just a muffled shuffling of movement, as if people were tiptoeing around him, not wanting to disturb him.

The room was bright. Too bright. Peter Furtado opened his eyes, or at least tried to. It hurt too much, so he stopped. He could feel the rest of his body, so he assumed he'd either survived the collision or he was dead and just waiting for St Peter to open the Pearly Gates to allow him in.

There was a smell.

He recognised it, but he wouldn't have associated it with either scenario.

It was a smell from his youth, and then from his freshmen year at college. Actually, it was a smell that had followed him around for many years, even into his marriage. But it had nothing to do with death or with Heaven.

It was semen.

It was a smell every boy knew intimately.

It was strong, heavy, cloying. He opened his eyes again. *Screw the pain,* he thought. If there was a sex smell and he had been out of it, then he wanted to know what it was and where it was coming from. He tried to sit up.

That hurt too.

It was only then he realised he was lying down and he was cold. *Am I naked?* This thought brought mild panic. What was happening to him? He wasn't the type to be interfered with, and there was no way he would take it lying down. He struggled, attempting to move his arm. Agony shot through his bones, actually from the inside of bones, as if the marrow inside them was burning. It was the worst pain he'd ever felt. Even worse than when he'd fallen from his motorcycle, shredding the back of his leg. He'd thought that would be the end of his flying career, but he'd manged to work through it.

Just like he'd work through this. He wasn't the quitting type.

The surface he was lying on was hot and getting hotter. He could feel his skin prickle as the heat continued to climb.

He tried his eyes again.

This time, they opened.

He began to scream as the figures he'd sensed in the room with him came into view.

5.

'WHY DID THEY take you?' the colonel asked after waiting for a pause in the patient's tale. 'How did they take you?'

Lewis couldn't see the man's face; he was still in the shadows, and the bandages covered most of it. What little he could see looked pale and scarred, like the face of a monster in a silly horror movie, the kind that were becoming so popular with the kids of today. *No wonder the world is going to hell in a handcart,* he thought.

'The impact was sudden, and it was complete. We lost all communications instantly, and we were spinning out of control. We had our suits on, and we were ready to decompress ...'

~~~~

'What is that thing?' Mallon asked as he gazed out of the window.

'Forget guessing what it is and fucking steer us out of the way of it,' Furtado snapped, shouting to be heard over the klaxon blaring in the small module.

Mallon turned to look at him. His face, through the helmet, was serene, calm. His eyes were accepting of what was happening to them. Furtado wanted to grab him, to shake him out of whatever malaise had gripped him. He turned to look at Green.

He wasn't moving. His head was resting on the dials, and there was a crack in his visor. There was no hiss or sign of any leakage coming from it, but still, it looked perilous. Furtado scrambled towards his colleague as Mallon turned back to the controls of the ship.

Green's eyes were open and moving. *He's alive, at least,* Furtado thought as he grasped at the man's suit, pulling him upright in his chair. 'Green. Green, can you hear me?' he shouted over the blaring alarm. He turned back to Mallon, who was now fighting with the dashboard of the out-of-control ship. 'Can you shut that thing up?'

There was blood inside Green's helmet. Not a lot of it, but enough to be concerned this high up in space with no communications.

'Sir!' Mallon shouted.

Furtado ignored him as he attempted to rouse Green.

'Sir, I think you need to see this.'

Furtado let go of Green, who flopped back in his chair. Mallon was pointing to one of the gauges. It was touching the red.

'I don't need to tell you what happens if that goes into the red, do I?' Mallon said.

Furtado shook his head, then bit his lip.

An unholy bang rocked the ship, flinging all three of them across the module and into a bulkhead.

The last thing Furtado saw before his own world went black was a limb. It was floating in the zero-gravity of the ship. The blood

120

that was spilling from it didn't fall; it just formed bubbles and followed the arm through the air.

Furtado couldn't tell whose it was. But for some reason, the image made him smile.

~~~~~

'What was the bang?' Lewis asked. 'Were you fired upon? Was it Russians?' He was standing now. The urge to shake this man before him was strong, but he knew he wouldn't, or shouldn't, touch him, not in the fragile state he was in. If he did, he would lose any trust the man had for him—also, he might lose his ability to relate his story.

He sensed rather than saw the patient's grin.

This angered him more than it should have. *Is he teasing me, playing me somehow?*

'The bang was exactly what you feared it was,' the patient said, his voice quiet, adding to the wet gargle that it was. The warble didn't sit right with the colonel's ears.

'What does that mean? What do I fear?'

The patient didn't answer.

'Tell me what the bang was. That's an order, Captain.'

The grin was sensed again.

'What do I fear?' Lewis almost shouted.

The patient remained quiet.

6.

AGONY. TERRIBLE, AWFUL agony.

Something was burning into his flesh. It was hot, concentrated, and it was moving.

Captain Dave Mallon, engineer on the Hermes IV, was wide awake as the knife—or whatever it was—cut through him. He could feel every moment, every agonised movement of the flaying that was happening to him. His body tried many times to blank out, to draw a curtain around what was happening to him, and to lose itself into sweet oblivion. Something wouldn't give him any quarter; it wouldn't afford him that luxury.

He couldn't move.

Not even his eyes would move.

They stared straight up, dead ahead, into whatever the bright light that was shining down on him was. He could feel whatever was cutting him, but he couldn't feel anything else. He couldn't move his head, or his arms, or his legs. Hell, he couldn't even flex any of his muscles.

Paralysed, was his only lucid thought as whatever was cutting through him continued its hot, then cold path.

He tried to move his head again. He tried to scream, but his mouth no longer worked. He couldn't even move his tongue.

His eyes were stinging, which was a strange thing to think about as something was slicing him to pieces, but it was a genuine thought. He couldn't blink, and the light shining down over him felt as if it were burning into his retinas.

He tried to concentrate on the light, to drown out the searing of his flesh as whatever and whoever it was continued to cut into him. He thought about the mission, the *failed* mission. He thought about his wife, his unborn child nestling in her womb, waiting to come out into a world with no daddy.

He wanted to cry, but of course his tear ducts were not working either, and even if they were, he couldn't move his chest to build up a sob.

An odd noise took his interest.

It gave him something to focus on, to take away from the world, *no, the universe* of pain that was consuming him. It was a welcome distraction. He turned his head to look to where the sound came from.

Only he didn't.

He couldn't.

Had the sound been in his imagination? Was he lost in some fevered dream? Was he wallowing in a Purgatory of his own making?

These were questions he welcomed. Anything to distract from the intense torture his paralysed body was enduring.

There was a whisper.

It was only faint, or at least he thought it was faint. This not only gave him something to think about, to concentrate on, but it made him realise his ears were working. He could see, he could feel, and now he could hear.

The whisper came again. This time, it was louder. Whoever it was, they were close, almost at his side. He had no way of knowing if he was standing up or lying prone on a bed somewhere, but he now knew he wasn't alone.

This time, a voice came. It wasn't a just whisper anymore, but it wasn't something he could understand either. It was a foreign word, if it was even a word at all. It sounded like a burst of white noise, like static on a radio.

He thought it might have been his ears adjusting when it came again. It hurt his ears, or his brain, or *something* in his head. It wasn't words. There was no structure to it. It sounded crazy to him in his severe agony, but there were no letters, no inflections, nothing but the ugly, white, static sound.

A shadow passed between him and the light. His eyes attempted to follow it but couldn't. Another sensation passed through him. It was his heart. He could feel it thudding. It was an odd sensation, as it didn't feel like it was thudding in his chest where it was supposed to thud. In his scrambled, messed-up state, he put it down to disorientation, to the agony of the cutting playing with his signals …

Until he saw it.

A human heart passed by his eyes. It was still attached to thick arteries, and it was dripping a fluid, a thick, viscus liquid. It hovered over him before moving on.

He screamed then. Or at least he would have if anything in his body was still working.

He didn't scream from the pain, he didn't scream from the vision of his still pumping heart passing before his eyes, he screamed at what he saw holding the organ.

7.

'WHO DO I fear?' Colonel Lewis asked. He'd calmed down now, realising that the patient wasn't playing with him, he was just confused. He'd been through real trauma. He was the captain of the module. A crew of three had taken off successfully, but only he had returned, three years later. He could only imagine what the Russians had done to him in that time.

'Do you fear me?' Furtado asked, his frigid voice nothing more than a whisper.

Lewis shook his head. 'I don't fear you, but I do fear what you might have told the enemy about our work.'

The patient laughed. It was an ugly, wet sound.

'What's so funny?' Lewis asked.

'The enemy?' the patient asked from the shadows. 'Why do you fear the Russians so much?'

'Because they want to destroy us. They are a threat to global power.'

'Do you not consider that they might think the exact same about you?'

Lewis shrugged.

He sensed the smile again. It felt like tentacles slithering up his arms, clutching at his flesh, tickling it with malintent. 'Do you not consider anything … *bigger* to be your enemy?'

'China?' Lewis gasped. He was just about to stand up, to go and report these findings to his superiors. Their biggest fear had just come true. The Chinese were taking that long-awaited step into the Cold War. This would have profound consequences on the outcome of this subversive conflict.

The patient laughed again. 'You are so paranoid, aren't you?'

This got the colonel's back up. 'How dare you talk to me like that? I'm a colonel. You would do well to remember that fact, Captain.'

'What makes you think I was talking about *you?* You're not the centre of the universe, no matter how much you think you are or you desire to be. You're insignificant little … *dots.*'

'Dots? What are you talking about, man? We have more military might than both those Communist countries put together.'

The ugly sigh stopped him in his tirade. *The fucking balls on this guy,* he thought.

'It's not about military might. It's not about who has the biggest *dick,*' Furtado whispered. 'It's about bigger stuff than that.'

'What's bigger than the military might of a nation?'

'You are a shallow people. There's more to you than this. You are small, pathetic, insignificant.'

Lewis's blood was boiling. He'd been told to allow the patient some leeway after everything he'd been through, but this was going too far. As far as Lewis was concerned, it was tantamount to treason.

He stood, his fists clenching. He could feel his fingernails digging into his fleshy palms.

The patient laughed again. The throaty warble returned and churned the colonel's stomach. He could deal with prisoners who had been brainwashed; he could deal with people who had fought to keep who they were but had ultimately given in. He'd seen many of them. But someone who had turned their back on everything that had brought them back from the brink? That was a line he was not willing to accept.

He gripped the door handle, needing to get out of this stuffy room, to get some fresh air and some daylight.

Furtado laughed again. 'Look at you, with your smallminded simplicities. You can't see, never mind deal with a bigger picture, can you, Colonel Lewis? You are so minute that you are not even *in* that picture. You or your mighty US of A.'

Lewis turned then, so fast his head went a little dizzy. 'Listen, Furtado. I've been told to allow you leeway, but if you're going to keep talking like this, then that leeway will be gone before you fucking know it,' he spat. His face was turning red, and his anger caused red dots to appear in his vision.

'Who are you calling Furtado?'

That was the last straw. Lewis turned and left the darkened room. As he went, he took Furtado's thick, wet laughter with him, echoing in his ears.

8.

LIEUTENANT GREEN HAD been an ace pilot since the age of sixteen. His father had been a pilot too, one of the great pioneers of aviation. His father before him had been a pioneer of the automobile, so it only made sense that he would end up as a space mission pilot.

He had grasped the opportunity with both hands, never let go, and excelled in his field.

His training had made his father proud, it had made his wife proud, if sick to her stomach, and it made his little girl proud to see her daddy doing what he did best, being a hero.

That was all he could think about now as he lay on the bed. His body was almost numb, and he knew what that meant. His grandfather had spent the last days of his life paralysed from the neck down. He was lucid enough to talk, and Green remembered him telling him that he could feel his body, he could feel when people touched him, but could do nothing about it. He told him that he thought it was just muscle memory, but it was the darndest thing.

Young Adam Green had always thought this was just his grandfather telling tales, trying to make him feel better about being made to hold his hand.

He would have held it anyway. He'd loved his grandpa.

This was what he imagined the old man had experienced.

He could see, hear, and smell. The stink in the room was ugly. It reminded him of his older brother, who had stuffed a wet sock in his face when he was a child. He never knew what was on the sock at the time, but it stunk like this room. He'd since found out, and although they laughed about it now, it sicked him at the time and had been the cause of many a fight between them.

Right now, he couldn't even feel pins and needles in his limbs, but he could feel a different, odd sensation. Someone or something was rummaging around inside him. It didn't hurt, at least not physically, but the thought of what was happening pained him psychologically. He could feel himself being reduced. Parts of him were being removed. He didn't know how he knew, but he did.

He was less of a man than he had been before they'd left Earth.

He wanted to shout out. He wanted to thrash, to rage at whoever it was doing this to him, but he couldn't. He could hear the metallic rattle of what he thought of as instruments being placed down on a hard surface. He could hear strange bursts of static, like an untuned radio or the end of a vinyl record when the needle never auto-returned.

It sounded like communication, as there were replies that even his primitive ears, *if I even have ears left,* could differentiate as different pitches and speeds.

All he could see was a bright light, but he could also make out shadows passing by the light. He guessed they were the *bastards* who were working on him.

As another rough hand rummaged around inside him, removing things, moving things around that had no place to be moved, he cursed the Russians. It could only be them. No one else would be barbaric enough to do something like this to another human being. *Well, except those bastards during the war,* he thought.

This thought was not pleasant. His own uncle, and his grandfather, both on his mother's side of the family, had been killed in POW camps in Europe. His thoughts went out to them and what atrocities had happened to them.

Nazis ...

This thought was too much for him. Were the Nazis back? Was this their bloody revenge for their losses during the war?

The static communications continued to chatter. He was now convinced it was talk, but he could hear no structure, no words, no sentences. Just short, cold bursts. He could tell they were excited about something, as the bursts were coming shorter and faster, with little or no space between them.

Even though he wanted to know what was happening inside him, when it stopped, when he could no longer feel anything moving about inside him, it scared him more than anything he had ever been scared of before. He didn't like what was happening right now. It had gone quiet, too quiet. The static bursts had stopped, and the silence was throbbing in his head.

Having absolutely no sensations happening to his body was worse than having someone violating him. It felt as if it were a total absence of ... everything.

He could still see the lights glaring down at him. He wanted to blink, to moisten his eyeballs, to clear them, but he didn't have the capacity to do that. He was a vegetable. Unable to move, unable to speak, yet he could see, and worst of all, he could think. *At least the bastards haven't taken* that *from me* ... The word *yet* sprang into his head, and he struggled to rid it. He didn't want to think about what was to come.

That was when he saw another shadow move between him and the burning lights. He wasn't alone after all. For some reason, that comforted him and petrified him at the same time.

The shadow stopped moving, but he could sense it was still close.

It moved again, and he saw it ...

His brain, as he felt like that was the only part of him left available to him, screamed.

It screamed, and screamed, and screamed.

As the world slowly dimmed, Alan Green was still screaming.

9.

'RUSSIANS, CHINESE, GERMANS … you have so many words to describe your very own species. Don't you realise that you are all just leaves on the same tree?'

Colonel Lewis was leaning against the door behind him. He wanted to flee again, he thought he needed to, if only to get that horrible warbling sound of the man's voice out of his head. He didn't want to hear what he had to say; he didn't need to listen to the madness spewing from the man's mouth. *The poor bastard,* he thought. *They must have really done a number on him. He's totally lost it.*

'You have exactly the same DNA, the exact same genetic makeup. You are all humans, just the one species, only slightly different variations.'

Lewis didn't know what this man was warbling on about. DNA? He didn't even know if that was a word or an acronym. All he did know was that he was talking rubbish. He had *nothing* in common with those Russian bastards, or the Chinese. *Or those coloureds,* he thought. *They look nothing like me. They're completely different.* He needed to get this man's insane ravings out of his head; he needed to distance himself from this situation.

I need a cigarette.

'Colonel Lewis,' the throaty warble said from the enshrouding gloom. 'We're not finished, are we?'

Lewis closed his eyes and banged the back of his head on the door. He thought he was finished; he hoped he was finished. As far as he was concerned, this *freak* could rot in this room. There was something about him. Something he couldn't put his finger on. But he creeped him out. The colonel was not a man to be roused by something as intangible as creepiness—he was a ranking officer, after all, and normally cut an imposing figure. Yet there was something about this man, something ... *more!*

He turned to face the door. He gripped the handle and began to turn it.

Captain Furtado, born in Idaho, married, two children, a clean and exemplary record, began to laugh again. Lewis's hand went limp on the handle. He wanted to turn it. He wanted to get the hell out of there. He had an irrational urge to run. Apart from the exercise he did on a daily basis, he couldn't remember the last time he'd run from anything. All he knew was that he didn't want to be in the presence of this man anymore. He didn't want to smell his stink. It reminded of him of something unsavoury. A smell from his youth, the smell of the bedroom.

'Colonel Lewis!'

The unexpected voice made him jump. He let go of the handle and opened his eyes, too fast for comfort, to see the doctor opening the door and entering the room.

'I'm sorry, Colonel, did I startle you?'

Lewis shook his head. 'Not at all, Doctor. I was just going … I needed a … erm, a comfort break.'

The doctor was nodding, then he looked at the clipboard in his hand, almost as if he was surprised to see it there. 'Erm, well, it seems there's something you really need to see. I'm not sure how it's happened, but there might have been a mistake. That's not Captain Furtado. We think it's Lieutenant Green.'

'You *think* it's Green?'

The doctor chewed at his cheek as he looked at the report on the clipboard before him. He was shaking his head. 'I can't explain it. His bloods came back as Furtado's, but take a look at this.'

He handed the clipboard over to the colonel. There was a smile on his face, but it wasn't a happy one.

The doctor looked troubled.

10.

THE SHADOW CONSUMED the small module. *Engulfed it* might have been more appropriate. The darkness dwarfed the spacecraft. The Hermes IV had absolutely no chance against it. The larger ship had barged into the smaller one, crippling it, sending it out of control.

It damaged the ship beyond repair.

It damaged the crew beyond repair too.

A panel in the bigger ship opened. The hatch had been hidden within the smooth, imposing hull. A light shone from inside, and the Hermes IV was pulled into the darkness of the larger ship's depths.

Once it was inside, the hatch closed again.

The module had been swallowed by the behemoth that was overshadowing it, as were the three critically injured crew members inside it.

11.

ADAM GREEN WOKE. The bright lights were no longer glaring down upon him. There was no more rummaging around in his stomach, and there was no more numb sensation. He could feel his arms, his legs.

He blinked his eyes, stretched his mouth, and stuck out his tongue. He hummed, just to make a noise.

He flexed his fingers, bent his knees, and moved his head from side to side.

There was no pain, just a strange *oddness* he couldn't identify.

~~~~

Dave Mallon woke. There was no more cutting sensation. The cold agony that had caused him such discomfort was gone. He felt fresh, alive, healthy. He could feel his body—it was an odd thing to think, but it was such a good thing to experience.

He blinked his eyes, stretched his mouth, stuck out his tongue. He hummed, just to make a noise.

He flexed his fingers, bent his knees, and moved his head from side to side.

There was no pain, just a strange *oddness* he couldn't identify.

~~~~

Peter Furtado woke up. The lights that had been burning into his retinas were gone, as was the paralysis he had succumbed to. The torture of not being able to move, the anguish of living the rest of his life as an inert *thing,* a burden on those he loved and those he had vowed to protect, was gone. It, along with his spirits, had been lifted by a small feeling of pins and needles in his arms and legs.

He blinked his eyes, stretched his mouth, stuck out his tongue. He hummed, just to make a noise.

He flexed his fingers, bent his knees, moved his head from side to side.

There was no pain, just a strange *oddness* he couldn't identify.

12.

'SO, THAT'S GREEN in there?'

The doctor huffed.

'What? It's a simple enough question.' The colonel looked at the door to the patient's room. He had felt it better to discuss this outside the earshot of the injured man.

'It's not the simple question that's vexing us. It's the complicated answer.'

'I can handle complication, Doctor,' Lewis snapped. 'I'm a big boy.'

The doctor was shaking his head. 'OK, then, the answer is yes, that *is* Green in that room.'

'What was complicated about that?' Lewis snapped again. He was losing patience with the good doctor, and this conversation. This whole situation, if he was being truthful.

'I haven't finished, sir. *And* ...' the doctor continued, 'the answer is no, that's *not* Green in there.'

'I don't have time for riddles, Doctor.'

'It's not Furtado or Mallon either. Yet at the same time, it is Furtado *and* Mallon.'

Lewis's anger was wallowing somewhere dangerously close to the surface. 'I don't have time for this stupidity.' He turned away from the doctor and grasped the handle of the door.

'That's a chimera, Colonel. That's not any of the crew who left in the Hermes IV, yet it's all of them, all at the same time.'

The sound of warbled laughter coming from the room on the opposite side of the door chilled his blood.

No, it did more than that. It froze it completely.

It wasn't just one laugh he heard.

Now he understood the warble, he understood the ugly throaty voice he had been talking to. He understood the man's insight into humanity.

It wasn't just one man.

~~~~

The thing that stood before them was tall. Its body was slim, barely humanoid, and from what they could see, it was naked. Its red-hued flesh looked to be almost liquid as moisture shifted below its surface.

Its head looked like it should be too heavy to be supported by its thin body, yet it was, and effortlessly too. Its huge, dark eyes looked insectoid. Hundreds of smaller eyes inside the obsidian holes, each blinking independently of each other, stared out. There was no nose to speak of, and what looked like the undulating lines of an instrument measuring light or sound waves as a mouth.

The men, who were now just one man, looked at the being. They had become used to its appearance, accustomed to whatever species this might be.

The short, sharp blasts of static were now words to them. They understood the cadence of the language, the linguistics, the formations of sentences within the noise.

'Today is the day you return to your planet,' the alien said. 'We know you understand it was an accident that caused our union. We were observing your species, determining if you were ready to join the greater community. However, you are not. Your individual lives were in danger from the collision, and we had to work fast to repair you. Some parts of you were already dead, and we couldn't use them. We did the best we could with what we had.'

The creature smiled. They understood the concept of this creature's facial features.

'It's time for you to return. Your message shall be one of peace and understanding. Your species can only evolve if you understand each another, if you love one another and embrace your subtle differences. Once you do that, you will be eligible to join the greater community and embrace everything it has to offer.'

The men, or what was now *the man,* stood. They were happy to be going home, but they would miss the welcome they had received from these people.

Their only hope would be that the people of Earth would listen to their message. That they would understand and they would grow, like *they* had, and learn to love, not to hate. It was a message they would carry with them and preach to whoever would hear it.

They had been given a chance to heal. Now, it was time for them to heal the rest of humanity.

Three in one …

A trinity.

13.

COLONEL LEWIS WAS no longer alone.

Twelve men, including the doctor, were behind him. All of them were armed; all of them were scared.

As the door opened, Furtado, Mallon, and Green, all of them fused into one body, stood to greet them. They held their arms out as if to embrace their fellow humans, to offer them the chance to gaze upon their evolution.

It was the first time the colonel had seen the full extent of the man. It was uncanny. It was ugly, gross, an unholy aberration of humanity. The Russians were obviously more advanced than they knew, and they were also more savage. How could anyone do this to another human being, to three human beings?

It was disgusting, and it was wrong on every level.

It needed to be studied.

The travesty needed to be destroyed.

'Are you ready to learn, to grow, and understand your fellow men?' the thing asked in its wet, alien voice. 'We have such wonders to show you.'

A single gunshot rang out in the room. It deafened the colonel, leaving him with an ugly high-pitched whining noise in his head.

A small hole appeared in the abnormal head of the naked thing standing before them. Its eyes narrowed as it looked at the men before it, making and holding contact with every other man's eyes in the room.

It fell back into a sitting position on the bed behind it.

Just before it died, a single tear welled up in one of its eyes and trickled down its scarred, imperfect, inhuman face.

It was all over for this creature.

Its future would now be endless studies, dissection, to be picked apart by scientists, doctors, military strategists. There was no way those Russian bastards were going to have more advanced techniques than the good old US of A.

Not for long, anyway.

DE McCluskey

DE McCluskey has been writing for almost ten years now. He was a late bloomer after thinking he was going to make it big on the rock 'n roll scene, then the stand-up comedy scene, then he thought he would be a computer professional ... but after finding out that all of those things involved really hard work, he decided to take the easy route of becoming an author. You know, the life of lounging about and not really doing much!

He started his journey writing comics and graphic novels before moving on to novels and novellas.

He can be found all over social media, mostly Facebook and Instagram.

THE CHIMERA'S EMBRACE
Matt Holland

Chimera

Now

NATHAN'S LEG HURT. Nathan's leg always hurt, but today was the worst it'd been in some time. Rain was always a problem with the pins holding it in place, but he'd walked further on wetter days than this with no trouble.

It could've been because the last time he'd pushed himself out of his comfort zone like this was the day he broke his leg in the first place. And today he wanted the exact same thing that he'd wanted all those years ago.

Nobody looked up at him, a soggy stranger, as he limped to the bar. Most of the clientele of the pub were old, tired men who just wanted to be left alone. They sat apart at round tables, chasing down mouthfuls of peanuts with swigs of warm beer as they stared at the football match playing out on the dusty TV on the wall.

The only friendly face belonged to a large golden retriever that came trotting up to Nathan, wagging its tail. Nathan drew his leg back to keep the dog from bashing by accident and patted the friendly creature on its broad head, receiving a gentle lick on the wrist in return.

'What's yours, pal?' The bartender was a squat old man with biceps like overripe melons. He narrowed his eyes at Nathan as if he was trying to work out if he was a cop or not. If the dog put

Nathan into his comfort zone, the bartender yanked him back out again, leaving him stammering and confused.

'Hi, yes. Sorry, erm,' Nathan studied the beer taps as if he could read them through the haze of panic descending around him. 'Could I have a whisky and soda, please?'

Nathan had no idea where that came from. He'd never drank a whisky and soda in his life.

The bartender sniffed and picked up a soda gun that looked like it hadn't been washed since Major was prime minister.

'Second thought, just the whisky, please,' Nathan said, which confused him even more, since the last time he'd drank straight whisky, he'd thrown up for over an hour.

The bartender poured by eye, not even measuring the whisky he sloshed into the glass.

'Two quid, mate.'

At least the place was cheap. Nathan paid with a fiver and didn't ask for change. 'Thanks. Is Burt in?' He tried to sound casual, but his voice squeaked on the word "Burt."

The bartender jerked his bald head behind him, where Nathan could just make out a dark corridor off to one side of the bar.

'In the snug, mate,' he said.

'Cheers.'

Aside from the Philharmonic and a couple of the older pubs down south, Nathan had never seen a pub that still had a snug. He made his way around the bar, stooping over a little to duck under a small doorway. The corridor looped around to a bright, cozy room with a fire roaring in one corner. The pins in Nathan's bad leg seemed to melt into the bone as he approached the fireplace, like it was seeking out the warmth.

The golden retriever from earlier trotted past again, dropping on its haunches next to a wiry scarecrow of a man hunched over the fireplace. The man reached out with a hand that looked like a tree branch, scratching the dog behind the ears.

'You were asking about Burt?' he said in a thick scouse accent.

'Yes, is that you?'

'That depends on who's asking, doesn't it?'

The man, presumably Burt, wasn't a pretty sight. His skin was tanned and wrinkled like he'd been shaped out of leather, with a long nose extended over an eggshell-coloured beard that hung to the middle of his scrawny chest. A battered pork pie hat was perched on his liver-spotted head at an angle that might've seemed jaunty on a younger face.

Nathan wasn't sure what he'd been expecting. Long velvet robes with stars and moons embroidered on the surface? A bubbling cauldron full of newt eyes and rat tails?

'Names have power, lad,' the thin man went on. 'Tell me yours and what you want Burt for, and maybe I'll help you find him.'

'"Nathan.' As he spoke, Nathan got a strange feeling like he'd just put his hand on a stove he didn't realise was still hot. The feeling passed before Nathan could properly examine it.

'And what's her name?'

'I'm sorry?'

'The woman. The one you're here for.'

Nathan froze, thoughts scattering to find purchase on anything he could say. The old man read the look on his face and laughed in a way that showed off his blackened teeth.

'It's always a woman.' He motioned to a chair across the table from him. 'Either that or money.'

Nathan lowered himself into the chair. The smell wafting over from the other side of the table was sweet, like icing sugar with a faint hint of almonds.

'So, which is it? Money? Or a woman?' The old man took a long swig from the fizzy amber liquid in his pint glass, ice cubes banging against his remaining teeth.

Part of Nathan wanted to give the old man the wrong answer. Tell him that he was here for money. Keep him on his toes, assuming he had any.

But Nathan was only here for one reason. Lying about that reason had never made him happy. The truth was his best option here.

'It's a woman. Her name's Maria.'

Maria. Just saying her name made pleasant tingles run up and down Nathan's spine. Her name, her face, the way she smiled; they were all things he wanted to lock away out of sight and never think about again. Nothing good could come from his obsession with her.

And it was an obsession. He made no illusions about it. What else could it be?

But Nathan couldn't control his dreams. That was the hell of it. The more he tried to force her from his mind, the stronger the dreams became.

Nathan would dream of sitting with her in a quiet pub. Or sharing a train ride together. Or maybe it was a memory of the two of them back in school—altered for a better ending. They'd talk together. Nathan never remembered what they talked about, but he knew that it was deep and meaningful. Learning the secret parts of each other that neither could share with anyone else. Sometimes they'd hold hands. In his dreams, Maria's hands were always warm.

He'd dream these silly dreams of his every night and wake up aching in the chest like he'd just been punched in it.

And so, her face was in his mind almost every day. Her name was the first thing to swim up to his lips in the morning. No matter how much he tried not to think of her, Maria was always lurking.

Nathan didn't want to tell Burt about the dreams. The snug of the Hare and Hound was Burt's place. The dim light, flickering fires, and that sickly smell in the air all belonged to him. If Nathan brought his dreams into this world, he'd be corrupting them somehow. Just saying Maria's name out loud here was bad enough.

The old man put his empty pint down with a satisfied smile. 'Thought as much. You'd think more folks would come through here asking about money, what with the economy and all, but no. It's always a woman. Sometimes a man. But mostly, it's a woman.' He leaned forward, the crackling firelight throwing long shadows across his toothless grin. 'Well, now that we're all acquainted, how can old Burt help you?'

'She's ... that is ... I ...' Nathan stuttered. He couldn't find the words to even begin explaining this. He never could. He reached for his glass, only to find it empty, but he couldn't remember ever taking a sip from it.

Maybe that was why the place was so cheap. Booze that drank itself.

Burt nodded his head as if he read meaning into every one of Nathan's confused, stammered words. 'I see. That bad, eh?'

'It's not fair to her,' Nathan said. Burt cocked his head to one side to listen. 'I mean, we barely speak to each other. She probably doesn't think about me at all.'

Burt held up a hand full of bony fingers. 'Before we even discuss business, you should know I can't make anyone fall in love with you.'

Nathan flushed red at the thought, whether from anger or embarrassment, he didn't know. 'Of course not. I wouldn't ask for that.'

Nathan didn't want to think about what he would've done if Burt had offered to force her to fall in love with him. He hoped he'd be just as outraged.

From Burt's smile, Nathan could tell he was thinking the same thing. 'Of course not. I can't control people's minds any more than I can control their bladders, and believe me, get to my age and you have enough trouble controlling your own.'

'Your bladder or your mind?' Nathan asked.

Burt gave a high, wheezing laugh that sounded like steam escaping a locomotive. He slapped one of his bony knees, making the golden retriever tilt its head in confusion. 'Hah! And here's me thinking you were a sighing little romantic without a sense of humour. That's good, that is. It'll help you with what's next.'

'What's next?'

'What's next is we get some more drinks. You don't start a pact like this sober, I'll tell you that for nothing.' He leaned back in his chair and called over his shoulder. 'Dickie!'

The same squat bartender from before appeared in the door to the snug. 'You two all right in here?'

'All good, lad.' Burt rattled the ice cubes in his empty glass. 'We'll need another perry, and whatever my friend here is having. He's paying, of course.'

'Of course,' Nathan agreed. Considering what he was here for, a round of drinks was the least he could offer as payment. Especially if the second round was as cheap as the first.

Dickie sniffed and lumbered back to the bar, leaving Burt and Nathan alone once again.

'So, this Maria,' Burt said. Nathan didn't like him using her name. Just hearing it out loud from someone else made him feel ashamed for even mentioning her. 'How long have you known her?'

Nathan had to do some quick calculations in his head. 'Twenty years or so.'

It was actually just over nineteen, but Nathan thought it best to round up. It sounded more impressive, like it was an actual relationship.

Burt's eyebrows went almost to the brim of his hat. 'Twenty years? You can't be more than twenty-five.'

'I'll take that as a compliment,' Nathan said. 'I'll be forty this year.'

Burt shrugged. 'Anything under sixty is still a pup to me. So, you've known her a long time. You never thought to just ask her out?'

As if Nathan had never thought of that, often. Almost every day. 'That's what I'm trying to do.'

'So, you just came to me for courage, is it?' Burt leaned back in his chair, one hand scratching the golden retriever behind the ears. 'That's a little disappointing, to be honest. I thought this would be something more.'

'I'm not afraid.' Nathan didn't know how to phrase the request, and it was beginning to get on his nerves. He knew what he felt, but when it came to explaining it, he either sounded like a deranged stalker or a babbling fool. He certainly felt like a mix of both. 'I've asked people out before. I can do it. It's easy. That's not the issue. The issue is …'

God, what was the issue? How did he even phrase it?

'If it's a performance issue, I can get you some little blue pills. They sort me right out, let me tell you.'

'No,' Nathan snapped, perhaps a little sharper than he'd intended. 'No. Maria is someone I knew from school. Every time we spoke, I got so tongue-tied I could barely form a sentence, so I never told her how I felt. We didn't talk for years afterwards, and we only started to reconnect before … you know … the C-word.'

'There are a lot of c-words. Especially in this context,' Burt said.

'The Coronavirus. We were starting to get to know each other again. I was starting to come out of myself and actually have conversations with her, then bang, we get quarantined for a year and a half, and now we're out again, I'm that same stuttering idiot I was back in school.' Despite the roaring fire, Nathan's leg hurt. He glanced down and saw that his hands were gripping his thighs so hard the knuckles were white. 'I want to ask her out, but I'm worried all she'll see is that same fat, awkward weirdo I was in school and not the fat, awkward weirdo I am now.'

It was a bad attempt at a joke. and Nathan only went for it because he suspected Burt was about to chime in with the same thing.

They were alone in the snug, except for the golden retriever. But even so, it felt appropriate to lean in closer to Burt and whisper. 'I've heard you can do things.'

Burt's mouth worked up and down as he sucked on his gums. 'You're not the first to come to me looking for a love potion—'

Nathan recoiled. 'What? No. That's disgusting. I don't want to force her to fall in love with me.'

Burt cracked a smile. Or as close as he could get with the teeth he had in his head. 'I'm glad you said it first. Some of my customers don't half get the hump when I tell them love potions don't exist. Well, they do, but they're called Rohypnol, they only work for one night, they're illegal, and I don't sell them.'

Being offered Rohypnol was worse than being offered Viagra. 'That's not what I'm after. All I want is a fair shot, win or lose. If she says no, fine. I can move on with my life.'

'Then I'm still struggling to understand what it is you want.'

'If I ask her as I am now and she says no, I'll always wonder if it's just because she remembers what I was like in school. I can't ask her as I am now. What I want from you, if you can do it, is to make me the type of man that's perfect for her. And after that, we can let the chips fall where they may.'

155

~~~

Then

'Gemma Templeman,' said Owen.

Nathan had read the word "crestfallen" before, but he'd never seen it demonstrated so perfectly as by Greg in that moment. His eyes widened, and his jaw hung open in a wide 'O' shape.

The three of them sat on the wall outside the school library, away from the noisy football match and the quiet smokers. Just the three of them, munching sandwiches and telling secrets. Secrets like what girls they liked.

Greg recovered quickly. 'Me too.'

Nathan didn't get it. It seemed like everybody fancied Gemma Templeman. She was thin and blonde and was always going out with whoever the cock of the year was at the time. At that moment, it was Steve Bradshaw, but she'd broken up with Robbie Prince a few months earlier, and before that, it'd been Jimmy Webster. All the boys fancied her.

Everyone except for Nathan. Nathan only had eyes for one girl.

'What about you, Nate?' Owen asked, desiccated remains of a ham sandwich still clinging to the roof of his mouth.

Nathan wondered if the girls ever talked about the boys like this. If they did, he wondered if he, Owen, and Greg were ever mentioned. He doubted it. Owen and Nathan were two of the fattest boys in the year, and an old rumour that Greg never showered, had followed him from primary school. Nobody was going to admit to a secret crush on one of them.

Least of all her.

'Oh my god, look at his face! It's gone bright red!' Greg laughed.

'No it's not,' Nathan tried to protest as his cheeks heated up. He didn't want to talk about her with these guys, saying her name out loud at all, even in a whisper, might make her hear it and find out how he felt.

At twelve, that seemed like the worst thing in the world.

'Come on, lad. We told you ours,' said Owen.

'It doesn't matter. I don't like anyone.' From the way Nathan's face was burning up, he doubted either of his friends would believe him.

'It's just us here, mate. Nobody else is listening.'

It was true; they were alone on this side of school. Most of the others were either still in the dinner hall or playing football around the corner. Only weirdo nerds hung around the library at lunch time. As one of those weirdo nerds, Nathan felt as safe here as he ever felt anywhere.

He took a deep breath and steeled himself as if he was about to go to war. 'Maria,' he said, so quiet he wasn't sure he'd even said it out loud until he saw Greg and Owen's faces both change. 'Maria Fontana.'

There were no other Marias in their year, but it still felt important to say her surname too. Just to be on the safe.

'Eeee, no way,' Greg said. 'She's weird, her.'

'That's weird, that, Nate,' said Owen. 'She's a bit heavy, isn't she?'

Nathan was furious at them both for dragging it out of him just so they could make fun of her. Considering that Owen was fatter than Nathan, it was a bit rich for him to be criticising anyone's weight. Besides, who cared what size she was? She was beautiful and smart and interesting. And, so what if everyone thought she was weird? All those things that other people thought were weird—the pale makeup and dark lipstick, the homemade jewellery she always wore, the dolls' heads she had dangling from her backpack, the way she was always reading, how she was the same age as Nathan but she seemed to know more than some teachers—these were all things Nathan found fascinating. He wanted to know everything about her.

He wanted to say all this, but all he could think to say at the time was: 'So?'

Not very eloquent or honest. But neither Owen nor Greg had an answer. So, they ate in silence until the bell rang to bring them to their afternoon classes.

~~~~

Now

'Playing around with fate can get real weird, real quick,' Burt explained. 'So, you need to understand the rules to keep that weirdness to a minimum.'

'I see.' Nathan shivered. The air was cold in spite of the fireplace.

'For starters, I need a way to commune with her spirit. Do you have something that belongs to her?'

Nathan didn't know that he had to bring anything. It felt like he'd just sat down to an exam he hadn't studied for.

'Don't give me that face,' Burt said. 'This isn't so hard. Lots of things belong to us that we don't really think about. Our ideas, our shadows, hell, even a photograph will work.'

'Does it need to be a physical photograph?' Nathan asked

Burt shrugged. 'Picture's a picture, innit?'

Nathan took out his phone and scrolled through the pictures on his Facebook profile. Lucky for him, he didn't have many. He skimmed past the memes, awkward selfies, and photos of nights out until he found the one he was looking for. The one from March 2020.

It was a candid shot of maybe a half dozen people all packed in on one long table. Nathan was sat at the end, closest to the camera. A big, beaming smile on his face. The face of a man who'd had just enough pints to drown his self-consciousness but not enough to be an embarrassment yet.

There were two women on the opposite side of the table to where Nathan was sitting. One had bright red hair and was leaning back as she laughed at whatever Nathan had been saying.

He wished he could remember what that was. Especially because of the other woman at the table.

She was a dark-eyed woman with ink-black hair swept back across one shoulder. One hand was raised up to cover her plump, smiling lips—as if she was trying to hide her laughter from the others. The other hand was reaching out for the glass of red wine between her and Nathan.

Maria Fontana. That expression on her face had haunted and thrilled him for over two years. She was laughing at what Nathan was saying. In that moment, that single sliver of time, she was enjoying his company.

Nathan couldn't remember much from that night. Only that Nathan and his friends had bumped into Maria and her friends by accident on a night out. Normally, something like this would send Nathan scuttling for cover like a cockroach in the light. But he'd been at that good level of drunk where there was no awkwardness. No arguments. No explanations or excuses. They hadn't even mentioned the cemetery. Just two people reconnecting honestly after a long time.

This, right here in this photograph, was everything Nathan wanted. If anything in the world could explain what it was he was trying to get, this was it.

He held it up to Burt. 'Will this do?'

Burt scratched some more tangles into his mop of a beard as he studied the photograph. 'That's her, eh? If I may say, she's real pretty. I can see why you like her. I've always had a bit of a thing for redheads.'

'What? No. It's her.' Nathan pointed Maria out, being careful not to accidentally flick to another picture.

'Oh, really?' Burt sounded disappointed. 'Not my type, but takes all kinds I suppose. Yeah, this will do. And you're here too, so I won't need a picture of you. Best crop all those others out, though. Don't want to tangle their fates in with yours. WhatsApp it over to me when you're done.'

'Sure.' Nathan went to work slicing the other people out of the photograph. He'd finally narrowed it down to just him and Maria when he realised something. 'Hang on, you use WhatsApp?'

'"Why shouldn't I?' Burt said. 'Got to keep up with the times.'

Nathan sent the photo over to the number Burt gave him. Part of him felt like the biggest creep in the world, but the rest of him wanted that night back so bad he didn't care. 'Anything else I need to do?'

'Hand over the money, of course.'

Nathan had almost forgotten that part. He fished the envelope with the agreed payment out of his jacket. Five hundred pounds. It didn't sound like much to have a fate rewritten, but there was a peculiar weight to the envelope as Nathan handed it over. As if the amount had not only been tripled but also converted to pennies.

Burt snatched the envelope into his jacket, but not before letting the golden retriever at his side take a sniff, like he was asking the dog for permission.

'That's where your job ends and our long, long night begins.' Burt drained some of the yellow liquid from his glass.

'How long does it take for me to notice any changes?' Nathan asked. Perhaps too late. He was beginning to think he'd just been swindled by a con artist and all of this was just silly.

'Impatient, aren't you?' Burt said. 'But yeah, I suppose after twenty years you would be. I don't know when the changes are

161

gonna happen, that's not my area. Folks usually notice results inside of a week. Sometimes sooner.'

'What should I expect?'

'Who knows?' He sounded more impatient now that he had the money. It wasn't helping Nathan's buyer's remorse. 'But I can tell you it'll happen overnight. One night you'll go to sleep, and when you wake up, things will be different. At least that's what I've heard.'

'You don't seem very certain,' Nathan said.

'Oh, I'm not. Fate works on its own schedule. If you find that you get no results at all, come back and see me this time next week.' He flashed a gummy grin. "Then again, maybe you won't get any results at all? Maybe you're already the perfect man for her?'

He cackled at that. A true dry-throated cackle that sounded like a rusty motorcycle juddering into life.

Nathan was starting to suspect that nothing would happen at all. The internet ad and those testimonials had been an elaborate lie; the only change to Nathan's life would be to his bank balance. He'd come back in a week and find the snug empty and Dickie the bartender telling him there'd never been a person called Burt in the first place.

Nathan knew all of this. But something inside, some deep-seated instinct—perhaps it was sheer desperation—wanted to believe.

'Thank you, Burt,' Nathan said.

'Oh, I'm not Burt.'

That instinct shut itself up quick. 'I'm sorry?'

'I'm not Burt. My name's John. This is Burt.' He scratched the back of the dog's head.

The golden retriever looked up at Nathan, tongue lolling out of one side of its mouth.

'What?'

'Burt's a fae creature from the world between worlds, aren't you, boy?' John said, scratching Burt behind his ears.

The dog yawned so wide it gave a little squeak as its jaws closed.

'Are you kidding me?' Nathan said.

'We don't joke about these sorts of things, lad!' John said.

'I think—' Nathan reached out, already preparing to ask for his money back, when one of the golden retriever's paws shot up, slapping into his palm. As if they were shaking on the deal.

Nathan could've sworn the dog winked at him. Must've been the whisky he couldn't remember drinking.

~~~~

Then

'We heard you fancied Maria.'

The voice made Nathan's heart crash up into his throat. It was Vicky and Nicki, two girls whose rhyming names betrayed how inseparable they were. They rarely spoke to anyone outside of their little group, least of all Nathan. But one of the people in that group was Maria Fontana.

Nathan's cheeks flushed red. He wasn't sure how word had gotten to Maria's closest friends. Greg and Owen were the only people he'd told. It was supposed to be a secret. They'd promised.

One of them must've blabbed. But who? And why? Nathan hadn't betrayed their confidence. Their secret crush on Gemma Templeman was still locked away. Not that it would've been such a scandal; everyone fancied Gemma Templeman. They wouldn't be cornered in the school corridors and accused like this.

Nathan was too scared to be angry about it. If Nicki and Vicky knew, that meant it was just a hair away from getting back to Maria, assuming it hadn't already.

He was ashamed of himself for keeping it secret, ashamed of himself for telling Owen and Greg, ashamed of himself for feeling things for someone who would never feel the same way back.

'She feels the same way,' Vicky said.

Nathan stopped breathing for a second.

'She says she wants to meet you at the cemetery after school,' said Nicki.

Vicky turned her face away, either to cough or to laugh.

'After school?' Even after saying it out loud, it didn't seem real. It couldn't be happening.

'After school.'

Nathan allowed himself to get excited. He really did.

~~~~

Now

Nathan jolted awake and kicked at his sodden sheets in a panic. His legs got tangled up in the duvet, and he flopped out of bed like a landed fish.

He gripped at his bad leg on impulse, holding it closer to his body to cushion the impact. He took the full force of the fall on his back, punching the air out of his lungs and leaving him gasping and confused on the floor of his room.

He wasn't sure how long he lay there, but his alarm clock showed 3:55 in the morning by the time he'd collected his thoughts and found the strength to haul himself up to his feet. It was depressing being up this early on a Saturday while still being sober.

The sun must've risen early because he could see through the darkness without any problems. He lumbered to the bathroom down the hall to take a piss before attempting to go back to bed. He was yawning as his tired eyes drifted to his reflection in the bathroom mirror.

He froze at the sight of the thing staring back at him.

It had to be a trick of the light. Had to. It had to.

~~~~

Then

Nicki and Vicky had said to meet Maria at the cemetery behind school, which seemed in character for what he knew about Maria from their few conversations. She liked weird, dark stuff. Monsters and ghosts and bands where the lead singer looked like they'd just been exhumed from a crypt.

Even so, Nathan was sure he'd been at the wrong place. She didn't turn up the first night. Or the second. When Nathan had spoken to Nicki and Vicky about it, they'd always said Maria was just too nervous to show herself, but she was definitely going to be there tonight. Definitely.

So, Nathan was there, waiting in the pissing rain for the fourth night in a row.

He huddled for shelter under one of the droopy trees that overhung the cemetery gates. From there, Nathan had a good view of the whole cemetery, such as it was. From the tiny chapel in one corner to the stone angels that overlooked some of the gravestones. It wasn't a pleasant place even in the daylight, but the dark grey sky made midnight out of the late afternoon, and all Nathan wanted to do was go home.

It was too cold to be outside this long. He wished Maria would finally show up. He also wished that she wouldn't. Nathan wouldn't have to think of something clever and witty to say if she didn't turn up, but if she didn't turn up, he'd have to wait even longer for her.

He caught a smell of something thick and tar-like. Something that he'd later learn was weed smoke from a wet joint. A smell that would still make him feel sick many years later.

The gates creaked open. Nathan's heart tried to eject itself out his throat. His breath caught and his mind went blank in anticipation.

But it wasn't her.

Three boys entered the cemetery with the resounding slap of a hard leather-cased ball bouncing off the flagstones. Nathan had never seen any of them at school, but from their wide shoulders and scruffy facial hair, he could tell they were older than him. Sixth form students, maybe.

They kicked their football around the graves, passing it to one another when they weren't passing the joint. At the time, Nathan thought it was just a cigarette, but that was scary enough. Scarier than the prospect of whatever lay under those graves. That, more than anything else, told him he shouldn't be there.

Of course, Maria wasn't going to turn up. He was stupid to believe she would.

'Oi!'

Nathan was still doing his best to avoid looking at the boys, so he assumed they were talking to each other. He picked a spot, an angular grave off in the far corner of the cemetery and stared at it. Away from them. Just minding his business.

'Oi, fatty!'

There was a peal of laughter, and Nathan knew they were talking to him.

Nathan was almost grateful Maria wasn't here to see this.

One of the boys lunged out from between the branches. He was so tall, and his body odour, cheap deodorant, and lingering weed smoke formed a thick fug that made Nathan's eyes water.

'"What are you doing here?' he said. He had crooked teeth surrounded by a dark, tufty attempt at a beard.

'I was leaving,' Nathan said.

Another boy appeared behind him, even taller than the first. Even taller than some adults Nathan knew. 'You want to buy some weed, lad?'

'No, thank you,' Nathan said.

'Yeah, you do,' said the third lad as he strolled between the graves. This last boy was both tall and wide, with a broad belly that bounced with every step. He dropped the football to his foot and thumped it Nathan's way, too hard to be a pass. Nathan ducked, and the ball crashed against the tree, scattering branches down amongst the thick roots.

'I don't. I was just going home,' Nathan said. Nothing too bad had happened, but he could already feel the burn of the tears pushing their way into his eyes.

'You were waiting for us, weren't you?' said the wider boy, stomping on the ball before it could roll away.

'I wasn't.'

'"Who were you waiting for then?' said the boy with the crooked teeth.

Nathan didn't know what to say. He couldn't get the thoughts into his head fast enough to filter them down into words.

'How much money have you got on you?' said the tallest boy.

'I haven't got any money.'

'That's too bad because weed costs thirty quid. If you can't afford to pay it, you can't afford to leave,' said crooked teeth.

Nathan broke into a run, something a boy of his size probably shouldn't have been doing at all, but especially not when he was surrounded by three boys who were bigger and faster than him.

The very tall boy lashed out with a kick, catching Nathan high on the shin. It stung, but only for a split second. Only for as long as it took him to stumble. Only as long as it took the crooked-toothed boy to shove him over, one foot still tangled in the roots. Nathan's body went one way, and with a tearing, cracking sound, his leg went the other. A thunderbolt of pain struck Nathan so hard everything went black.

The next thing he remembered, the boys were gone, replaced with the swirling lights of an ambulance parked up near the cemetery gates. He was screaming and crying, and the pain was too much for him to focus on what the paramedics were saying. It hurt so much. And it kept hurting.

As far as he knew, Maria never turned up.

~~~~

Now

Nathan had never been a fan of looking at himself in the mirror. He never thought he looked how he should. He was always fatter than he remembered, always balder, his skin was always worse. Mirrors were a hard slap in the face every time he walked past one.

But a mirror had never slapped him as hard as this one did.

The first thing he noticed was his face. It was monstrous. His mouth and nose had elongated, dragging his jaw along with it to an almost wolf-like snout. Sharp little teeth were pushing out of

169

his gums, making them bleed a strange black blood. His eyes, usually light brown, were now glowing yellow. His torso was bigger and broader than it had been, so long that it actually added a few extra inches to his frame. As he'd gotten taller, his belly had receded. What had been flabby had now been replaced by row upon row of taut, wiry muscle.

Both arms were bulging with new muscle. Nathan's left arm, previously ending in a hand, now terminated in a set of long, slithering tentacles with suckers on the underside. Five tentacles in place of his five fingers.

Nathan touched his face with his hand—the one that was still a hand—and screamed at the sight of it. It looked like the hand had flattened and grown overnight, its long fingers topped with sharp half-inch claws that glistened in the half-light.

He staggered back from the mirror, favouring his left leg as he always did, the one that had gotten caught up under the tree root all those years ago. Previously, every step hurt, even on a good day. But this time, there was no pain whatsoever. The lack of it caused Nathan to overbalance and tumble out of the bathroom, flailing with both his new arms for balance.

He stopped short, hanging above the floor, one leg off the ground. His tentacled fingers had snatched out at least a foot away from his hand and glued themselves to the doorframe with their suckers. The tentacles were spread out wide, one tentacle grabbing each side of the door and two more wrapped around the top. Normally, getting up and down put strain on Nathan's joints, making him grunt with exertion whether he meant to or not. But now, the tentacles pulled him back onto his feet with alarming but strangely satisfying strength. If he hadn't felt his feet on the cold floorboards, he would've sworn he was flying.

This brought him face to face with his own reflection again. It wasn't as scary now he was used to it, but it still made his heart skip a beat.

He thought back to what he'd said at the pub. The specific way he'd asked Burt to rewrite his fate.

"What I want from you, if you can do it, is to make me the type of man that's perfect for her. And after that, we can let the chips fall where they may."

This had to be Burt's doing. It was the only thing that made sense. The chips had fallen. And apparently, Maria's perfect man was some unholy combination of wolf and octopus.

She had always liked darker things. Monsters and ghouls and meeting at cemeteries.

~~~~

Then

It was three months before Nathan could go to school again, another year before he could do so without a crutch. Previously, his afternoons were taken up with chess club, drama club, karate. But now he was at physio almost every night, exercising and straining his shattered leg until it had the strength to carry his steadily increasing weight.

He never spoke to Maria about it. Very rarely spoke to her again. They'd never been especially close, but Nathan was now actively avoiding her as much as possible. In their few classes together, he tried to sit as far from her as he could. When previously they'd said hello when they saw each other in the corridors, he now avoided eye contact with her altogether, pretending he hadn't seen her.

Nathan knew on some level that it wasn't her fault. But every time he thought of her now, he just pictured her laughing with Nicki and Vicky about how they'd tricked some dumb fat idiot into waiting like a sea widow at the cemetery every day. On his darker days, he almost believed they'd sent those boys into the cemetery to break his leg on purpose. It was absurd, but no more absurd than the idea that Maria might have had any interest in him.

They never even said goodbye to each other on their final day at that school.

Over time, the pain in Nathan's leg dulled to an uncomfortable background noise. It was always with him, but he was strong enough to walk without a crutch. He went to college, a university on the other side of the country. He had girlfriends and boyfriends, and none of them made him feel much of anything for very long. He got a job as a graphic designer and loved it.

He didn't think of Maria at all until March of 2020, when he'd spotted a beautiful dark-eyed woman on the other side of a pub and he'd been drunk enough to go and say hello. It was her, and she was beautiful and weird and funny, and they didn't talk about the cemetery or his leg or how he'd avoided her. They laughed and drank, and it felt right and good. They swapped social media details and promised to keep in touch, and a wound Nathan didn't even know he had started to close.

It was as if all his life, he'd been limping around an empty corridor full of locked doors he'd never even thought to look behind until Maria had given him the key. He didn't know what it meant, but he knew this was a person he wanted to have in his life, either as a friend or something more.

A few weeks later, they were all locked down in their homes and Nathan's dreams began.

~~~~

Now

Nathan spent the weekend like Gregor Samsa, huddled up in bed with the lights off, feeling like a large vermin and wracked with pains as his muscles and bones knitted themselves into this strange new shape.

He still couldn't believe this was Maria's ideal man. He'd heard of furries before, people who were attracted to anthropomorphic animals, he'd heard of people into tentacles—but never both at the same time. Never in this combination.

He supposed the world takes all kinds.

Once the growing pains subsided, Nathan could almost see the appeal. In his body, at least. For years, he thought a six-pack was impossible, the sort of thing only professional athletes and celebrities could get. But now Nathan's stomach had a genuine eight-pack, broad and powerful pectorals, shoulders and arms bulging with muscle that would make even a professional wrestler jealous.

But it wasn't just the body. His face had changed. At first, Nathan had thought the snout was wolf-like, but it actually seemed more feline than that. A lion or a tiger, perhaps. Not quite a snout, not quite a nose, but some hideous amalgamation of both. Then there were the fangs. The glowing yellow eyes. The fangs. The whiskers. And the fangs.

And let's not forget the tentacles he had on one hand. Tentacles that still made Nathan's skin crawl even though they were attached to his body.

On Monday, he called in sick from work. Said he'd tested positive for covid. He'd never had to call in sick before, so his boss told him to take the week and call again next Monday if he needed more time.

Nathan wasn't sure how he could ever go back there.

He was furious with himself. What had he been thinking? It was a dumb little high school crush. Their paths had gone in different directions. Maria was probably happy with her life, and butting into it would only complicate things for her. Nathan knew so little about her, but he'd still put her up on an impossible pedestal. Over what? A schoolboy crush and one drunken conversation he could barely remember. Not worth ruining her life over. Not even worth ruining his.

And Nathan had ruined his life. He couldn't see a way to see his friends or family again. He couldn't work. He couldn't even show his face in public. Even if there was somebody out there he could talk to, what was he supposed to tell them? How do you even begin to explain this?

To top it all off, he was hungry all the time. He'd eaten every scrap of food in the house by Tuesday. Nothing seemed to keep him full for long. He'd eat an entire steak, a whole pack of ham, every egg fried off into a massive omelette, bags upon bags of oven chips. Then less than an hour later, his stomach would ache and rumble again, howling for more food. He got so hungry he thought he might die. In his weakest moments, he almost felt like that might not be such a bad thing.

The only thing that kept him going was that he was currently wearing the body of Maria's perfect man. That had to mean something. He just had to figure out how to get in touch with her. Maybe once he saw her and explained what was going on, she might be able to help.

If this was what Maria was into, Nathan had it. But he still couldn't bring himself to message her. Too much time had passed. He'd need to find a way to bring it up naturally. But why would he be messaging an old school acquaintance he'd barely spoken to in twenty years?

"Hey, Maria. How's it going? Turns out I'm some kind of giant cat man with a tentacle arm now." She'd think he was mad even before he mentioned being a cat man.

Once again, he was putting too much on someone who was barely even an acquaintance. But it was the only direction he could think to move.

Nathan tried to come up with a plan as he worked on resolving his food problem.

Fortunately, a long period of lockdown had prepared Nathan for this. There were so many food delivery apps, all designed to keep humans from interacting with other humans. All Nathan had to do was put that he had covid under the special delivery options and he could have an excuse for coming to the door in a mask and gloves. So long as he kept his tentacles out of sight, most delivery drivers were happy to drop off a family portion of food to this one giant man. Especially when Nathan tipped above twenty percent.

Aside from the trouble he had squeezing his new, weird face into a mask, this went smoothly. He ordered breakfast, lunch, and dinner from different restaurants with different names because he still didn't feel right using his old one.

Eventually, the money would dry up and he'd have to think of something else. Especially since his boss wasn't quite as happy to have him call in sick that second week.

He still hadn't figured out what to say to Maria. He'd liked a few of her posts on social media, mainly about how stressed out she was working full-time while trying to write. He wanted to comment on these, but he didn't even know what she did for a living other than that she apparently worked lots of nights and weekends. There didn't seem to be any organic way to get a conversation going.

This was high school all over again.

He was beginning to think about just going outside and seeing what would happen. He'd wear a mask and hood, of course. And he'd keep his tentacles tucked away in his pocket. He found that the tentacles could grow and recede almost at will, to the point where he could hide them in his sleeve if he wanted. Maybe this new appearance wasn't as grotesque as he thought. Maybe nobody would care about a monster man lumbering up Bold Street. Maybe Nathan had passed a few monsters before and just not realised it.

So, on Thursday the 4th, he psyched himself up, stuffed his big feet into his old shoes, draped a hoodie over his bulky body, and got ready to leave the house. He was only going to take a quick walk around the block at dusk, twenty minutes at most.

Right after dinner. Which, on that day, he decided would be pizza. Four of them, all topped with as much meat as he could get.

When the doorbell rang, he did his usual routine. Hood up, covid mask over his snout, tip money in his right pocket so he could draw it out with the most normal of his two hands. By this point, he wasn't even thinking about what he was doing, it'd just become second nature.

He opened the door, and behind the stack of four pizza boxes was a curvy woman with pale olive skin and eyes as dark and beautiful as the ocean at night. Nathan's breath struck him in the heart like an uppercut.

'I've got an order for Joe?' Maria said, using the fake name he'd put on the order form.

The words he wanted to say were arrested in his throat. He couldn't even think straight. His chest constricted like it was being squeezed in a massive fist.

Nathan couldn't speak, but he acted.

He lowered his mask. He took his tentacles out of his pocket.

Maria blinked once, but aside from that, her expression didn't change. 'Huh,' she said. 'So you are real.'

~~~~

Later

It was one of those old people's pubs, the kind that always set Maria's nerves on edge. As soon as she walked in, every set of rheumy, cataract-clouded eyes turned to her, slithering over her as she approached the bar.

She slept in the arms of a man who was seven feet tall, muscles on top of muscles, and the only part of him not covered in coarse black fur was the tentacles on his left hand. Joe was what society would call a monster. Someone that should make you flinch if you saw him on the street. On balance, he was scarier than any of these dumpy old men.

And yet, these old men terrified Maria much more. Her stomach twisted and spun in knots as she pretended not to notice them staring at her. As scared as she was, she refused to show it, striding up to the bar with confidence. In Maria's experience, people pounced on any show of weakness. It was important to hide everything, even the good stuff, just so nobody got the wrong idea.

There was a short, squat man serving behind the bar. He had a careworn face and a warty nose. Maria warmed to him at once.

He grinned at her in a way that was both friendly and faintly off-putting. 'What can I get you, love?'

'I need to speak to Burt,' she said.

All pretence of friendliness dropped from his face. For a moment, Maria thought he was going to kick her out. 'Follow me, he said.

Chimera

He led Maria off the main bar and down a dingy corridor to a backroom. The type of place you'd bring someone if you were going to sacrifice them to some dark god. Maria had written a few stories about that, so she made a mental note of how the yellow wallpaper peeled off the bricks like flesh from a bone and the flickering lights tossed spidery shadows into the gloom. Good details to write into a story later.

The bartender pulled a curtain back, revealing a cosy room dominated by a large fireplace and a set of plush armchairs. Between them was a round table and a golden retriever, who looked up at Maria as she entered, wagging its tail.

'Burt, someone here to see you,' said the bartender.

The dog's tail wagged even harder, and a skeletal hand patted it on the head. 'Who is it?' said a rough voice from behind one of the armchairs.

Maria stepped inside. 'Are you Burt?'

The figure in the armchair turned towards her and smiled with a mouthful of rotten teeth. He was an older man in a short-brimmed hat, with a long, bushy beard. He was so skinny he looked like he'd blow away if someone turned a fan on. 'That depends on who's asking, love.'

The bartender slipped back through the curtain and returned to the bar, leaving Maria alone with the old man and his dog.

'I hear that you can change people's fates,' Maria said.

'Maybe I can, maybe I can't. Who's to say there is such a thing as fate, eh?' He barked a dry laugh. 'You still haven't told me your name.'

'Maria,' she said.

'Maria?' He furrowed his brow. 'I've not seen you before, have I?'

'No.'

'Hmm.' The old man sucked on his teeth. When he opened his mouth, Maria was worried he might've swallowed some. 'Very well. What can I do for you?'

'I need to find someone.'

'Have you considered going to the police? I hear they're good at that sort of thing.' He motioned to the empty chair, and Maria pretended to ignore it. She preferred to stand.

'They're not good at it. They gave me a crime reference number and said they'd get back to me,' Maria said. 'By all accounts, the person I'm looking for doesn't exist.'

The dog yawned, and the old man cracked a smile. 'I see. You know, normally, these conversations bore the piss out of me. Refreshing to have someone get to the point so quickly. Speaking of refreshing …' He picked up his pint glass and rattled the ice cubes in it.

Maria saw what he was getting at, but she pretended not to. 'Can you help or not?'

'Me? Perhaps. That depends on who this person is, what they were to you, who you are, and why they disappeared.'

'The person's name is Nathan Hill. He was someone I knew in school. My name is Maria Fontana, and if I knew why they disappeared, I wouldn't be coming to you, would I?'

The dog tilted its head up, and for an instant, he and the old man locked eyes. The old man turned back to Maria. 'I do believe we can help you. In fact, I'm almost certain we can. But first, satisfy an old man's curiosity. Why are you looking for this Nathan Hill?'

'It's stupid.'

'You know what is stupid? Making an old man crane his neck around like this just to talk to you. Take a seat, for goddess's sake.'

Maria sighed and made a big point of how much of an inconvenience this was for her. She sat down in the empty armchair; the dog crept over and planted its head in her lap. She scratched him behind the ears as she spoke,

'I knew him a bit when I was younger. He wasn't a total dick, but we weren't very close. I didn't really think about him at all until I bumped into him at a bar one time and we got on really well.' Maria caught her face loosening up, preparing to smile at the memories of that night. But she put a stop to that at once. 'Surprisingly well, actually. We swapped details that night, added each other on the socials—but then never spoke again. I kinda forgot about him until I met …'

Maria hesitated. The old man was listening. It looked like the dog was too. But revealing Joe's existence would put him at risk.

As much as she was worried about Nathan, he was just some weird guy she'd only had a handful of conversations with in her entire life. He seemed nice, but it wasn't worth revealing Joe's existence just to find him. Especially if Nathan didn't want to be found. He'd certainly gone through all the trouble of deleting all his social media accounts, school and work records. Even his parents claimed not to know who he was.

The old man derailed Maria's entire train of thought of thought with just two words. 'The Chimera.'

Heat rose up to Maria's cheeks at the mention of it. 'How do you know about that?'

'We who dabble in fate know of many things that lurk out on the fringes. Besides, this story reminds me of a book I read once. Maybe you know it.' The old man hauled himself up out of his chair and limped over to a bookshelf on the right wall. He was shorter than he'd looked while sitting down. Maria reckoned she was probably taller than him.

The old man retrieved a book, and dropped himself back into his chair, exhausted, like he'd just trekked around the world.

He tossed the book over, and Maria nearly fumbled it into the fireplace trying to catch it. She knew the cover, of course she did, she'd paid for it. That was her pseudonym on the front. The one she'd used during her monster erotica phase.

'*The Chimera's Embrace*,' Maria read aloud, frowning at the cover. It had never looked right. The creature on the front didn't match the one in her imagination. It looked more like a stock image of a werewolf with scales instead of fur. The one from the book should've looked like …

Well, it should've looked like Joe.

Despite that, it warmed Maria's heart to see the book again. Her copy had been gathering dust on her bookshelf for close to a decade, and you never saw it in book shops or libraries. She thought maybe ten people had bought the book during its entire run; that must've included the copy she now held in her hand.

'Why do you have this?' she asked.

'Had a young man in here a year or so ago. He … uh … mentioned he was a fan, so to speak. After he came in, I couldn't help but buy a copy for myself.'

'I see.' She didn't. 'And what did he want?'

The old man chuckled and stared into the fire. 'A love like the one in that book, if you can believe it.'

'I had no idea Chimeras were real.'

'Oh, they weren't. Not until a year or so ago.' The old man's smile deepened. The creases in his jowls had shadows growing in them. The dog's tail thumped from side to side. 'Maybe Nathan's happier where he is now. Did you ever think of that?'

So many things clicked together at once. The way Nathan had been at school. How awkward he'd been at the bar before he'd loosened up. Despite the warmth of the room, Maria's skin tingled with goosebumps. It wasn't hard to put together what had happened.

The old man nodded along with her thoughts as if he could see them too. 'For what it's worth, he didn't know about the book. If he had, he might've wished for something else.'

'What did he wish for?' Although Maria suspected she already knew the answer.

'It's not my place to disclose that. Speak to him about it, if you still want him back, even knowing what it'll cost you.'

Maria stared at the creature on the front cover. Nobody could get the Chimera right. Everyone imagined it differently. Maybe that was the point. Everyone saw what they wanted to see.

Perhaps that was why the book only sold ten copies.

Matt Holland

Matt Holland has been writing dumb little stories for over twenty years. His Gallaetha series was listed in the top ten best Urban Fantasy series on Amazon for about a week in 2012. His work has appeared in Cracked, the Escapist, and his own website Matt Holland Author Dot Com, where he's written a free short story every month since 2017. The first chapter of his upcoming novel *We Are Nobody* won a place in Writing on the Wall's 2023 Pulp Idol anthology. When he's not writing, he's either lifting weights, playing Dungeons and Dragons, appreciating real ale, or streaming video games on Twitch. He is weak against fire, lightning, and time, but strong against ghost-type enemies.

"Be careful what you wish for" is one of my favourite themes to explore in my writing. There's nothing I love more than an asshole genie that gives someone a twisted version of their own desires. "The Chimera's Embrace" is an exploration of this idea as well as the various ways we try to change ourselves for other people, particularly where love is concerned. Can you tell I'm also working through a lot of post-covid and high school angst as well?

THE CHIMERA PROJECT
Nick Valentine

I TOOK A deep breath and once again hit the Record button, planning to nail it this time. I spoke confidently into the camera lens, only glancing down to check my notes once in a while.

'We've known for years that genetic testing can identify inherited diseases within a person's genetic makeup, or DNA. However, ARTEK Labs is on the verge of discovering a way to make DNA malleable in order to remove or insert additional pieces of DNA without compromising its integrity.'

The notes, handwritten in blue ink from Doctor Holloway, had mentioned that I should pause here, but I couldn't really understand why. I continued.

'This will enable scientists like me'—here Doctor Einheart had written in red, *Pause and smile into the camera*; I certainly wasn't doing that—'to remove any inherited diseases or disorders within a person's genetic makeup and add parts of it to their DNA which might make them immune to illnesses, allergies, and perhaps even the process of ageing altogether.'

At this point in the notes, Doctor Holloway's blue handwriting proclaimed, *Try to create a sense of excitement and wonder*. My usually pale, freckled face blushed in sheer irritation. I knew he was trying to help, and I do like Doctor Holloway. He's well-mannered and kind, and he respects my opinion, but how in the hell was I supposed to create a sense of excitement and wonder? Exclaim "Wow!" and risk sounding patronising?

'The key to this process is the DNA's malleability; this will cause it to heal around these changes without the worry of rejecting a new DNA configuration.' I had been worried about this part because it's a gross oversimplification, but both Doctor Einheart and Doctor Holloway had assured me that it was more important for the potential sponsors to be able to understand it than to be scientifically accurate. It still pained me a little to not be completely honest with the explanation, but I persevered.

~~~~

At first, I flat out refused to do the video, until a sneering Doctor Einheart pointed out that it was actually stipulated in all our contracts that we could be used by the company, for the company in any matters regarding publicity, funding, setting a good precedent, saving face, etc ... The company had *really* good lawyers. I wouldn't have stood a chance.

'Within just a few years, we will be able to create super-soldiers with abilities the likes of which have never been seen before with relative simplicity, all thanks to DNA malleability. Once the process is perfected, we could attach the transparency and colour-changing abilities of the octopus to the skin of soldiers, providing them with the best camouflage imaginable.'

Doctor Holloway had suggested this part, though it had seemed to me an awful use of such an amazing discovery. 'It would never actually happen,' he had assured me, patting my shoulder with his caramel-coloured hands. 'The sponsors just really get off on the idea of super-soldiers.'

'We could eradicate cancer, heart disease, every allergy known to man, and give people the hard, thick skin of an elephant, the unbreakable bone density of a bear.'

The last note from Doctor Einheart advised, *Pause and wait for dollar signs to appear in the sponsor's eyes*. I took a breath. I was almost done.

'That's the dream, anyway, and it's getting extremely close to becoming a reality.' I pressed the button to stop recording and hit SEND. I sat back in my sturdy, high-backed office chair and looked around my small, state-of-the-art underground ARTEK Labs apartment. The once plain and smart white walls were now almost filled with scraps of handwritten notes in black ink and various brightly coloured diagrams of the DNA double helix broken down in various ways and from different angles.

I had just come back today after the four days of mandatory leave we had to have every three weeks above ground in the "real world" to stop us from going stir crazy (the labs, for safety and security reasons, are located quite deep underground), but I felt like this apartment was my real home. I hadn't really had time to get excited about being back, as I'd been too nervous about recording the video for the sponsors.

At least it's done now, I thought to myself. *I can finally relax!*

Suddenly, all the cool-temp daylight-coloured light fixtures gave two quick flashes, followed, as usual, by the ringing of the communication screens attached to both the main room wall and the bathroom wall; they both flashed pink to signify the mood colour of the person on the other end. I knew instantly that it must be Doctor

Einheart. He always showed up as pink.

I sighed heavily, got up, and walked over to the brightly lit bathroom. Whenever possible, I liked to take my video calls in there, as I could check my reflection first. I looked fine, but my frizzy ginger hair was a little unkempt. I have a tendency to run my hands through it when I get nervous.

I pressed the big round button on the wall near the mirror to answer the communicator. My reflection instantly changed to that of Doctor Einheart back at Sector B labs. There were lights flashing and alarms buzzing, everybody in the background was rushing to and fro, and I heard a security guard shouting about getting "the weirdo chief of security down here now."

~~~~

'Doctor Rochehart, what on Earth are you doing? Come to Sector B labs immediately!' He bristled. Beads of sweat had formed on his forehead. He was visibly shaking and angry.

I took a moment to revel in his irritation.

'I've only just completed and sent the video for the sponsors. It took me two and a half hours to get here from topside because of the trouble in Sector C labs …'

Sector C labs had been completely locked down this morning, and nobody had seemed to have any idea why. Things like that were always happening at ARTEK Labs. There was never a dull day, but it still irritated me to get stuck up in it and have my carefully planned out timetable ruined.

'Never mind that now. Sample VL is showing extreme

discrepancies since its latest treatment, and I need that brain of yours down here to recommend our next course of action,' he shouted, and I saw the large vein in his temple throbbing. I could tell from the picture on the screen that he was standing right outside the sample labs. When he had said "treatment," he was referring to the gamma radiation shower. He used the palm of his sweaty hand to wipe the sweat from his face while he waited impatiently for me to respond.

I wasn't technically on the clock yet and could leave him to sort out his own mess, but VL was one of my samples, and I really didn't want him fucking things up. 'Sample VL?' I asked, carefully pronouncing the letters. He nodded. 'What are the discrepancies?'

He looked at a chart he was holding attached to a clipboard and translated the reading from it. 'The temperature skyrocketed; the instruments are showing all kinds of nonsense about containment, even though the room is in full lockdown; rather than a radial degradation, the sample is showing an expanded mass; the—'

'Supercool the room right now. I'm on my way over there,' I told him, my mind already focusing on getting over there. I grabbed a white lab coat I had hanging from the wall like a bathrobe and thrust my arms into it.

'But won't that—'

'No, Doctor Einheart, it won't affect the structural integrity of the sample. Out.' I pressed the button to switch the communicator off and went out of the apartment door.

Luckily, the trouble in Sector C only affected you if you were coming from Topside. I'd be fine getting over to B labs from Personal Quarters. I got through the security checkpoint in record time, yelling and waving my pass around, and I headed for the tram station.

I was in such a rush I almost boarded train C31, which had a reputation for disappearances, displacements (people ending up in random places), and general weirdness. It was rumoured to have started because Sector C test labs were running experiments in time travel. I knew there was some truth to this. Of course, at the first sign of trouble, they had cancelled train C31 altogether, but after a while, it started turning up anyway.

I had accidentally boarded it around a month ago and passed out after the train seemed to start filling with a hazy green fog out of nowhere. When I woke up, I was in one of the labs in Sector C and I was told that it was two days *previous* to when I had boarded it. Apparently, this happened often since they started on the most recent projects. It was "nothing at all to worry about."

However, they needed to keep me in isolation for two days in Sector C so that I wouldn't run into myself in the next two days. This would have been a really bad time to have a repeat of that mess.

I had also discovered during an unofficial discussion with the chief of security that the green haze on the train had, in fact, been the result of one of Sector C labs' experiments in time travel. There had just been a minor mix up in computer coding for something and their "portal" had ended up stuck in the wrong place.

I waited for train C31 to automatically drive off and boarded train B11 instead; it had me at Sector B security front gate in about seven minutes. Roughly every quarter of a mile, there were security checkpoints where a person's identity was checked, as well as their current security clearance and any safety equipment/protective clothing they were required to wear.

~~~~

When I finally arrived at my lab, the place was in an uproar. Alarms were blaring and lights were flashing all around us; there were holes in the durastrength windows (which was quite a feat) and broken glass on the floor. Doctor Einheart spotted me almost immediately and made his way over in a flurry, pushing past a man in a security guard uniform with his hand bleeding.

'Doctor Rochehart!' he yelled over the sound of the alarms, which abruptly switched themselves off. He was still sweating profusely but looked much calmer than he had in the video screens. His face was flushed red with embarrassment. I crossed my arms and waited for an explanation.

'I was worried that the sample might be damaged by supercooling the room, so instead, I opted for encasing the sample in sub-terrafoam.'

I could feel my anger level rising and began to clench my jaw tightly.

'And how did that work out for you, Doctor Einheart?' I asked slowly in as calm a voice as I could muster.

'Urm, badly, I'm afraid.' He was looking down at his shoes like a naughty school child. 'But we've sorted out the problem, and now the sample is stable—'

'Because you supercooled the room like I asked?' I uncrossed and recrossed my arms. My clenched jaw was beginning to hurt.

'Yes,' he admitted quietly.

I had to try extremely hard not to call him a piece of shit.

'What happened when you encased *my sample* in sub-terrafoam, Doctor?' I snapped.

Sub-terrafoam was an oxygen free form mould made out of an organic clay-like substance that ARTEK Labs had invented because it never reacted with anything and was completely heat resistant.

~~~~

He stammered. 'The-the sample, that is to say, sample VL, somehow absorbed the sub-terrafoam casing and became volatile. It began to hurl projectiles across the room, injuring three, level two members of staff. It was then that *I* decided to supercool the room.'

'Doctor Einheart, are you telling me three people are injured because you decided you knew *my* project better than I did?' I tried to keep my voice calm but failed to do so.

'Had you been here doing your job instead of galivanting about making yourself look good for the sponsors, I wouldn't have had to make a rash decision without full knowledge of the project!' he retorted.

'I told you exactly what action to take, and you ignored me! I've been working on this project for three years. Who knows what kind of damage you might've caused? I'll be making a formal complaint to the administrator about this.'

If he responded with anything else, I didn't hear him because I immediately started checking the instruments in the room to see what kind of a state the samples were in. The instruments showed that at least half the mass of sample VL had gone—must have been fired off along with the sub-terrafoam. I left a message with security that anybody hit by one of the projectiles should be kept in Quarantine in case of contamination with the samples.

~~~~

Within the next hour and a half, thirty-two projectiles were retrieved from walls, tables, floors, and broken lab equipment. They still contained parts of sample VL, but, as they were also contaminated with the organic sub-terrafoam, it would be unsafe to join them back to the original sample, so I opened up a new file for sample AD— meaning After Discrepancy—and put it under observation in a separate lab, still supercooled.

There were still parts of the sample's mass missing, and I had a bad feeling they had gotten inside the three injured class two staff as shrapnel. Though they seemed fine and had relatively minor injuries, under my instructions they were each put into a chemically induced coma while we attempted to surgically remove the samples, and then subjected to CT scans.

I spent the rest of the day trying to discover why this strange reaction with the sub-terrafoam had occurred. I ran the process on computer simulations, analysing every aspect of genetic changes occurring in the sample. It seemed that the sample had reacted badly to its latest shower of gamma radiation, becoming volatile. It immediately rejected the sub-terrafoam, spitting all of it out as projectiles, but then once supercooled ... oh my god.

The sample had neutralised and become malleable! This was what we had been working on for years! We had actually done it!

In the projectile samples we had gathered and called sample AD, after supercooling, the remaining parts of VL had actually assimilated the sub-terrafoam genetic makeup, becoming stronger and near impenetrable. This was incredible! The cells were using the stronger parts of other organic cells to become more powerful and stronger without even having been programmed to do so.

The Chimera Project was more successful than I could have ever guessed it would be. I sighed heavily. This was great news, but I couldn't allow myself to celebrate. We had no idea what would happen to the three class two staff members that had been hit by AD/VL shrapnel. I decided to get over to Medical and see if there was any way that I could help.

~~~~

When I got over there, it seemed like good news. The CT scans showed every piece of projectile had been removed successfully and the shrapnel added to sample AD back at the lab. Obviously, I couldn't go into the quarantine room and see how they were doing for myself.

Instead, I made my way over to the security office at the back of the medical wing so I could watch the footage of them since they had been brought in. I figured I'd see if I could spot any sign of contamination from any remaining cells of VL.

I was friendly with Larry, the burly and eternally stressed-out looking security guard with a 1950s style moustache working at the small security office. The security offices were almost all identical in layout.

Once I explained the situation to Larry, he was able to get the ball rolling. He had to call the head of security for B and C labs to gain access to the previous footage so that I could watch it, but he assured me he hadn't noticed anything strange (though admitted he wouldn't know what to look out for).

I had met the head of security before when I had spent three days in C Labs due to the train mix-up.

Martin, who was usually referred to as "the weirdo chief of security," had been the one who had unofficially told me about the error in computer code which caused the train C31's unusual behaviour, but I don't think he remembered me, and he looked at me suspiciously when I told him I needed to view the previous few hours' surveillance video for the quarantine lab.

'I'm sorry, Doctor, but I can't authorise that without a very good reason,' he stated, giving me a very weird and out-of-place-looking toothy smile. I sighed heavily.

Larry appeared behind my left shoulder and pleaded, 'But, boss, it is *her* project. If there's any signs that anything is wrong with those people, she would know.'

He laughed dismissively to himself under his breath. He would take more convincing than that.

'You could be helping to save people's lives,' I told him. 'You do care about these people, right?'

He caught my eyes, and I could see perfectly clearly that he didn't give a shit about these people; in fact, I didn't think he could care less. But then he seemed to shrug it off and agreed that we could all watch the tapes together (he knew Larry had seen it already).

I got the impression he had decided to act like he cared.

Eventually, he wrote in the valid pass keys and the three of us watched the footage together on four times speed.

We watched as the three class two staff members, still in white lab coats, were brought into the large white quarantine room, which looked clean and bare, as though an ordinary room had all its furniture removed and had been scrubbed down with strong antiseptic chemicals. They were laid down on three separate stretchers that had been wheeled in, each about a metre's width from each other.

Instruments were waved over them, and each was given a shot to put them unconscious while they had shrapnel removed, and they were put under observation.

We watched as almost two hours passed on the recording with no signs of any contamination, but then their temperatures began to rise exponentially.

This took us back to real time, and as we turned our heads to view the live feed from the cameras, we watched the nurses and orderlies fuss around a little over them with ice packs on their foreheads. Then when their temperatures began to reach dangerous levels, three ice baths were dragged into the room.

My body felt cold and clammy all over, and I was frozen in terror. I almost wanted to run back through the corridor to medical and stop them on pure reflex, but my brain insisted that these people were trained for these types of things and would know better. I was wrong.

Larry, Martin, and I watched, transfixed to the screen, as six nurses/orderlies simultaneously lowered the patients into the ice baths on the count of three. Once they had been submerged, I screamed in horror at what came up in their place.

Their entire bodies had immediately begun to liquify. Their skin started pulsating and oozing; their entire bodies bubbled and expanded out of the tubs. My first thought was that they were no longer people at all but a monstrous unnatural mass. They had families. Wives and children. Then I thought of the other consequences this could have.

I ran down the corridor to the entrance to the quarantine suite, which was between us and the rest of Medical, and I immediately smashed at the bio-containment alarm with my elbow. The heavy containment shutter came down over the door immediately, and I could see through the viewing window that the shutter on the other side had also closed.

Two of the nurses in surgical masks came towards the door and started to pound on it with their fists, getting more panicked every second as they glanced back and forth towards me and the creature growing out of the tubs behind them.

I slumped down against the shutters, and all the mixed emotions built up in me. I started to cry, still hearing the occasional gasps and exclamations from the security guards, Larry and Martin, while they continued to watch the live footage of the security feeds.

~~~~

After what seemed like at least an hour had passed with me slumped there on the floor, Larry and Martin tentatively approached me from the corridor down towards the security desk. Larry was full of nerves and sweating as he waddled towards me, and Martin, who was usually so cool and calm, looked a little lost.

'It's some sort of creature. The whole thing merged into one entity, and it's smart; it knocked out the security feed. It will automatically reset in a few minutes, but I think we can assume everyone who was in there is dead.'

Larry crouched down near where I was sitting and murmured with a sad smile, 'You did the right thing, honey. God knows what would have happened if that thing had gotten out ...'

I nodded slowly.

'However,' Martin advised, 'we are a little stuck now. We can't get back to the labs except through Medical.'

'They can't see the camera feeds from the other end of Medical, right?' Larry interjected. 'So they don't know what's happened in there?' he observed when Martin nodded, motioning towards the door to quarantine behind me. 'What if they override security and let it out?'

Martin shook his head and retorted. 'They can't. After Doctor Rochehart here closed the doors, I inputted the necessary code to keep it contained there. They can access the feed, but only if they put an E-key into one of the security terminals. I could send them the feed from here. They can't let it out before I tell the computer it's safe.'

An E-key is an encrypted password on a USB flash drive. Only the highest-ranking staff had them. In B labs, that was Doctor Einheart and Doctor Holloway.

'The first thing we need to do,' I told Martin, 'is to get on the monitors and get in touch with the labs; let them know what just happened. If they can get Doctor Einheart and Doctor Holloway to one of the senior computer terminals, they can input their codes and burn this thing.'

All the labs in Sector B, as well as the quarantine room in Medical—because of the nature of the experiments that happened here—were equipped with a safety measure called a "Burn Switch." It was never used, for obvious reasons, but theoretically, if one of the experiments got out of control or became dangerous, the two most senior staff members (again, Doctor Einheart and Doctor Holloway) could insert their E-keys into a slot in the door and the room would immediately become engulfed in flames to neutralise any potential threat.

We went back down the corridor into the security booth, over to the screen, and typed in the number for the labs. It was answered after just a couple of seconds, and Doctor Einheart's severely stressed-looking face appeared.

He seemed to be in the middle of arguing with some nurses. He was red faced as though he had been yelling, and the forms of three or four nurses were visible to the left of him—two had their arms crossed over their chests, and one was crying.

'Ahh, Doctor Rochehart, where are you right now?'

'I'm at the security desk at the back of Medical and we—'

He interrupted. 'Ah, perfect. Get them to open the quarantine shields, will you? There's been some sort of fuss—'

'No, Doctor Einheart. There's been a serious incident. I think that it warrants for you and Doctor Holloway to use the Burn Switch.'

'Oh, what utter nonsense. Open the shutters and I will assess the situation myself.'

'No, Doctor Einheart. I'm sending you a section of the security feed so you can see what happened for yourself.' I nodded to Martin, and he played around with the computer behind me, cut out the necessary part of the security tape, and sent it to the terminal Einheart was using.

We watched as he took the USB drive E-key from around his neck and inserted it into the side of his terminal to view the security-protected clip, then saw his face change to an expression of first shock, then seemingly wonder and astonishment.

~~~~~

'My god!' he exclaimed. "We've actually done it."

'Well, in a manner of speaking, Doctor, but as you can see … this thing is dangerous,' I cautioned him. 'We need to get Doctor Holloway over, and the two of you need to burn the room, and we need to destroy all the samples of AV and VL because they will probably mutate too. If that monster got into the synthesised DNA we've been working on for super-soldiers—and merged with it—it would be unstoppable.'

Martin looked over at me with an open-mouthed stare.

'We still have all the data. We can easily recreate the samples again in more controlled conditions and fix the problem.'

Einheart thought for a moment and then slowly nodded.

'Doctor Rochehart?' Larry chimed, still sat at the security systems terminal. 'We're about to get the security cameras in

201

Quarantine back online. The system is resetting.'

I looked over at the screen, which was blank apart from the words: "offline. Reboot in thirty-three seconds … thirty-two seconds …" It was counting down.

When it got to "three, two, one—" the screen rebooted, showing the interior of the quarantine room of Medical. At first, I couldn't see the creature at all, but then my eyes caught movement on the top-left of the screen and I saw a limb of some kind being seemingly sucked into the ventilation shaft. It had already pried off its entrance.

I got back on the monitor to Doctor Einheart. 'Doctor Einheart! Problem! It's gone into the vent shaft! It can move, and it's strong!'

I heard a scream in the background of the monitor screen, and Doctor Einheart's face turned towards the sound with a look of panic and horror, then the video switched off.

Myself, Larry, and Martin all exchanged horrified looks for a second, then Martin panted, 'I can access the security cameras from here …'

He leaned over Larry and typed some commands into the computer, bypassing a series of password screens, before the security feed popped up. It was pandemonium. The room had been put on automatic biohazard lockdown, and there were people trapped inside with the monster. The monster had gotten bigger.

On the monitor's feed, I saw that, rather than a blob of flesh, blood, bone, and muscle tissue, it now seemed to have formed into a more human-like shape. It was devoid of any kind of skin but appeared to be held together with a thick, translucent film. It had two arms, two legs, and a head, all attached to a large torso, but all in all, the creature was at least eight feet tall.

I watched as the creature, surrounded by bodies, was shot at by security team members, who were standing between it and the remaining living staff members. I looked over at Larry and Martin. Larry looked close to tears, and Martin had his hand covering his face, peeking through his fingers, visibly flinching every time the monster was shot.

~~~~

Doctor Einheart was among the surviving staff members, standing at the computer terminal, typing frantically. His last act was to lock down the room and close all the air vents, trapping himself and the others in the room with the creature, for the greater good. Tears poured from my eyes. Maybe I'd thought too little of this man.

As it was shot, parts of the monster sprayed on the wall behind it, but as I watched, it seemed to reconfigure itself, filling up any holes in its body so that it wasn't being damaged much.

Then it jumped up and clung to the wall with large, serrated, knife-like nails and jumped at the remaining security guards, scratching and clawing at them until they each fell to the ground.

It killed the remaining staff members while they tried to scramble and pry at the door. All of them had been my friends and colleagues. I had to turn away when it killed Doctor Einheart.

After all the people were dead, it approached one of the bodies and kneeled over it. Hundreds of small fleshy tentacles burst out from all over its body and attached to the deceased, sucking it up into itself, assimilating it. It did this for all the bodies.

Its mass grew a little each time, and its insides seemed to rearrange themselves a little as they had when it had been shot by the security guards. Once or twice, it grew thicker limbs afterwards, and a few times its "skin" seemed to get thicker and change colour.

Every three or four bodies, it vomited out a thick red goop that looked as though it contained bits of blood, flesh, and bones. Perhaps rejected DNA?

Larry, still with tears in his eyes, turned up the volume on the security feed. Now that there was no one left to scream, we heard a low, deep breathing sound from the creature.

'We need to get in touch with the other parts of B lab, make sure they know what's going on.' B lab was made up of five areas. Areas One and Two were the different sets of labs used for materials, testing, and storage (the creature had broken into Area Two through the vents, but the lockdown had prevented it getting to Area One). Area Three was Medical, where we were now.

Area Four comprised animal testing labs (where we tested animals and extracted DNA from them in order to try and learn/copy their properties), and Area Five was disposal.

I typed in the numbers for Area One of B labs and waited for it to ring. Doctor Malcolm Holloway answered. He was old and dark skinned, with a small amount of white facial hair and thick black plastic glasses.

'Eliza! Thank God! We thought you were in there; I thought you'd been killed!'

'Hello, Doctor Holloway, it's good to see you too. How much do you know about what is going on?'

'Some sort of creature is loose in Area Two. Since it went into lockdown, I've been watching it on the security feed. My god, Eliza, it's incredible!'

'Us too. The first thing we need to do is to lock it down properly. When it was in Quarantine, it managed to get out through the vents. Doctor Einheart closed the vents when he locked down the lab, but it's stronger now, and I'm worried it could still break through.'

'Hmm, well, the vents have blast shields, but it would mean cutting off our oxygen. Let me run the maths ... Yes, we'd have approximately twenty-four hours of oxygen. Of course, once we've burned the creature, we can re-open the blast shields and get our oxygen back.'

'There's a problem there, Doctor,' I told him, my voice breaking with emotion. 'We'll need Doctor Einheart's E-key. It's in there with that creature.'

We both thought in silence for a moment. Then Martin proposed: 'I could synthesise a copy of doctor Einheart's E-key, but only from a main terminal, so I'd have to get to you, Doctor Holloway.'

'We're not letting you through there with that creature inside!' I snapped at him.

'There's maintenance hatches. It's a hell of a squeeze and it's only really used for rewiring, but it'll get me across the room. They should run right through Medical and both lab areas. I can keep in touch with Larry through security radio.'

Doctor Holloway spoke first. 'It's not perfect, but it's the only plan we have. How close would it put you to that creature?'

'It runs about a metre under the floorboards. Slightly deeper under quarantine.'

Something was beginning to bother me here. He was insistent that he had to do this and seemed eager to get away from Larry and I. It didn't seem quite the proper reaction, and he didn't even really seem scared, but in the absence of a better plan, I was stumped and let it go. Maybe this was why people thought he was weird?

'How do you get in?' I asked.

He pointed to a small panel built into the floor in the corner of the room.

'One of the security guards here can monitor your progress too,'" Doctor Holloway affirmed. 'Have you met Daniel Reid?'

The small walkie-talkie-type radio attached to Martin's vest gave out a crackle, then a voice sounded from it saying, 'Check. Check?'

Martin answered immediately. 'This is Chief Martin speaking. Is this Dan?'

After another slight crackle on the radio, Daniel replied, 'Yes, sir, this is Dan. I'm here with Holloway and some staff from Area One in Sector B labs.'

We saw a guy in a security team uniform wave into the screen from behind Doctor Holloway while talking on his radio. He was a tall, thin white male with slight stubble. The sight of him didn't exactly fill me with confidence that we would make it out of here alive. He looked like a rookie. I doubted he was older than twenty-five. For a moment, I forgot that he could see us on his screen, and I rolled my eyes.

Doctor Holloway spoke next from the communication screen. 'Don't worry, Doctor Rochehart, I assure you he's proven himself perfectly capable.' I covered my face with my hand, embarrassed. He continued. 'I've closed the blast shields on all the vents in B labs. We'll have approximately twenty-four hours of oxygen starting … now.'

We heard a slamming sound echoing from behind the ventilation shaft in the room we were in and a dull thud from the one next door.

We all instinctively looked back at the security monitors on the terminal to make sure the creature was still in Area Two labs. Martin locked the monitors on the creature so we could keep an eye on it. It was hunched in a corner of the room as if resting. Now and then, it seemed to shimmer as its DNA remodelled itself.

'If we're going to do it, it had better be now,' I concluded.

~~~~

Martin and Larry together opened up the hatch, and Martin crawled inside, with the walls almost hugging him. One of his hands touched the wall, and he let out a slight gasp. Larry put a comforting hand on Martin's shoulder and quavered. 'You have an injury? Are you sure you're okay to do this?'

'I'll be fine,' Martin asserted.

There were lots of wires and panels poking out at him, and he had to be very careful to not get himself tangled up in them. He just about had enough space to shine his torch around if he held it close to his body.

On Martin's instruction, Larry awkwardly closed the panel once Martin was firmly inside. After a few seconds, Larry's radio crackled. 'It's opened out a little now, but there's another tight spot ahead as I start to get underneath the floor,' Martin said.

A second or two later, we heard Dan answer with 'Roger.'

After around twenty minutes, the radio crackled again with Martin's voice. 'Underneath medical now.' We heard a low growl coming from the creature on the monitors.

We all held our breaths.

After a few minutes, the radio crackled again, but there was no other sound from it. Then the creature growled again, louder this time.

'It can hear the radio,' Larry whispered.

The radio crackled again, and Martin blurted, 'Approaching Area Two labs.'

This time, there was no sound, but the creature rose up from where it had been sitting. It seemed to stretch it's huge, clawed arms, then leaned its head down to the ground and moved along the floor like a dog sniffing at something.

'Fuck! Should we tell him it can hear the radio?' I whispered.

'God no,' bawled Larry. 'With those claws, it could tear him out of the floor in no time.'

Nothing happened for a few minutes, then the creature suddenly stabbed its giant claws into the ground and started tearing up the metal floor like a dog digging for a bone.

It continued for a few minutes as if ravenous, then suddenly stopped as though it had gotten its prize.

I cried silently for a few minutes over Martin.

I could see small tears in Larry's eyes too. 'He was a weird guy, but cool, y'know?' he whispered almost to himself.

I nodded.

'In training, he was ten times better than all the other guys, but nobody really hung out with him because of his weird interests. Serial killers, medieval torture techniques, stuff like that ... and he hated his name. Martin Tep—'

The radio let out a loud crackle, cutting him off mid-sentence. Then Dan's voice came through, saying, 'We've got him.'

Larry and I both gasped. I lunged at the radio on Larry's belt and asked, 'Martin? You've got Martin?'

It was Martin's voice that answered. 'Yeah, I'm here. Sorry, guys, I figured out it must have heard the radio, so I left it behind. It almost killed me trying to get it. I'm making a new copy of Doctor Einheart's E-key on the SecurEkey app now.'

Larry and I put our arms around each other comfortingly, then Larry pulled the radio close to his sweat-covered mouth and moustache and shrieked, 'Martin, I have to say, you scared the hell out of us back there! Eliza and I are really glad you're okay.

'Thanks, Larry. Just a normal day in this place, right?' he replied.

This definitely wasn't a normal day.

~~~~

Within about an hour and a half (we kept our eyes on the creature the entire time, and Martin kept us updated of the progress on his newly procured radio), they were ready to burn the creature. Martin's voice crackled over the radio. 'I'm inserting both E-keys now. It will burn nonstop for ten minutes, and once it's done, the sprinklers will come on and the room will begin to cool. I'd give it about a half hour before making your way through.'

Larry started to look even more nervous than usual. He turned to me and warbled, 'Why is he inserting both the keys? Is Holloway not there anymore?'

'He probably just misspoke,' I mumbled.

We saw on the still-locked camera feed that some attachments on the ceiling moved, pointing downwards, then the room started filling up with fire. After that, the cameras shut off again, and all we could see was blank screens.

We heard the creature screaming, but it slowly died down, and with it, I felt relief flooding through my body and a calmness overcoming me. It was over.

'I just want to check something,' Larry breathed.

He typed a few things into the computer, and a list of installed apps appeared on the screen. 'Goddammit!' he barked.

'What is it?'

'Look, I don't know what it means, but the SecurEkey application is installed on this computer. He could have made a copy from here.'

I looked at him, aghast. 'So … why didn't he?'

'I don't know. But something weird is going on. I'm going to make us an all-access pass, just in case.'

'Isn't that out of your clearance?' I queried.

'Yes, but I can hack around the security measures.'

I looked at him with newfound respect and thought for a moment, then murmured, 'Do it. We've got nothing else to do while we wait for the room to get to safe levels.'

We tried to get through to Martin on the radio once or twice, but there was no answer. After the burning finished, we heard the vent blast covers open and fresh air started to pour in. We waited until the security camera in Area Two labs was back online before trying to get out. We didn't want to take any chances that the creature had survived.

When it came back online, we were greeted to the very welcome sight of a big pile of dust where the creature used to be.

Larry tried to look at the other camera feeds for the other parts of B labs, but they all showed as "Rebooting," as did the communication screens. He explained that might just be a security measure tied to performing a burn of one of the rooms.

We walked through the quarantine rooms of Medical; Larry used his pass to get us through all the doors. The only evidence of the creature was a large pool of dried blood. This was discarded DNA, as I'd concluded earlier, and shouldn't be dangerous, but we made sure to avoid it anyway, just in case.

We got through the door into Area Two labs, and there was ash everywhere from the parts of bodies and clothing discarded by the creature. The biggest pile used to be the creature itself.

~~~~

As we walked over to the door into Area One labs, I started to get a bad feeling. Why hadn't we been able to get in touch with anybody through the radio? Why wasn't anybody here waiting for us?

As soon as we opened the door, we got our answer. Larry vomited immediately. There were dead bodies everywhere. Not only dead but some were ripped apart; some had even been impaled with parts of metal piping from the ceiling.

I covered my eyes in sheer disbelief. Larry knelt on the ground, crying and whimpering openly.

We walked around the entire Sector B labs in silence. Nobody but the two of us were left alive. Even the animals in the animal testing labs had been slaughtered.

We found a computer terminal amongst the chaos, and Larry started to type things in. He pulled up the security feed for the Area One labs from around the time Martin had made it back.

We watched him getting congratulated for getting through the maintenance shafts without being killed, then he sat at this very terminal and started making a copy of Doctor Einheart's E-key. Then he left the room, and we followed his progress through the labs using the other camera feeds, greeting people along the way.

At one point, he stopped at another terminal, and Larry whimpered, 'Look, he's disabling the security measures!'

He got into Area One labs storage and located samples VL and AD and poured the contents of their petri dishes into his mouth.

He convulsed but didn't change form.

I remembered when I had entered Sector B labs during the havoc that Doctor Einheart had caused by disregarding my orders to supercool the sample. He had pushed past somebody in a security guard uniform with an injured hand, but none of the patients in the infirmary later were security guards; they were all class two science staff members!

We watched as he was approached by one of the level two staff. He grabbed at him and seemed to bite into his neck like a vampire sucking out blood.

'He's absorbing new DNA through the blood rather than simply assimilating the whole thing!' I rasped.

After a few seconds, he released the (now dead) staff member, and his entire form seemed to shimmer. For a moment, it seemed like he was taking on some of the physical characteristics of the dead man, but then, with some concentration, he seemed to right himself and become Martin again.

The next time he ran into another person, he was faster and stronger. He killed mercilessly. He made his way around the labs, absorbing all the DNA he could get his hands on, including the synthesised DNA we had been working on for experiments in making super-soldiers.

It wasn't long before he was able to kill in seconds and move faster than the camera could pick up. He showed as a blur, sweeping through the labs, killing everyone in sight.

We saw him take the copied E-key from the computer and contact us on the radio while he had his arm through the chest of Doctor Holloway.

He wrote "VLAD" on the wall in blood before leaving the Sector B labs, still killing anyone he saw. Then we watched him on the camera feed boarding train C31.

When we got the footage up from around twenty minutes ago from the next camera feed, he had disappeared.

'Shit. I know where he is,' I yelped. Because about a month

ago, I had boarded train C31 by mistake and been teleported inside Sector C test labs in the past, and I'd had to stay there for two days so I wouldn't run into my past self.

Almost two days ago, I spent two hours getting to my personal quarters because Sector C test labs had been put on complete lockdown.

'Larry, I think I might know what happened in C labs two days ago,' I told him.

Epilogue

WHEN THE SECURITY team (led by Larry) explored C labs later, they discovered, as we had expected, that everyone was dead.

Larry told me the rest over dinner a few days later.

Martin had appeared at the lab after disappearing from train C31, murdered everyone in sight, and escaped through an experimental time portal. 'I can't believe it. He seemed weird, but just like a regular guy! He was right here with us, and we didn't know what he was planning ...'

I nodded. I was still shaking from the whole ordeal, even days later. 'Yes, but how much of it was him and how much of it was because he was infected with AD/VL? I guess we'll never know.'

'Luckily, his escape obviously wasn't world-ending, as they are pretty sure the portal would have dumped him out the other end sometime in the fourteenth century,' Larry told me in between mouthfuls of his new, healthy, vegetable-based diet. (He hadn't been able to eat any meat since we saw the carnage left by Martin in C labs.)

'What was Martin's last name?' I asked him.

'Something foreign, uhm ... Tèpes?'

I put my hands over my head. He had hated the name Martin, so he had changed it. 'The samples were called VL and AD.

'Vlad Tepes was Vlad the Impaler,' I told Larry in utter shock and awe. 'A fourteenth century mass killer that the Dracula mythos is based on ...'

'Larry ... I think we just created the entire Dracula mythos ...'

Nick Valentine

Nick Valentine was born in the UK in 1988.

This is his debut published story.

His main influences include HP Lovecraft, Edgar Allan Poe, Graham Masterson, and Darren Shan.

THE CHIMERA OF AMELIA SWANN

Catherine Cavendish

AMELIA WAS MY special friend. Not that I saw her every day or anything. Only at Christmas when my parents and I went to stay with my widowed maternal grandmother. Granny Linden was my mother's beloved Mama. To the outside world, Honoria Linden was the epitome of Victorian society. Born in 1862, the daughter of a minor aristocrat, Sir Gerald Swann, she had married beneath her in society's parlance. Gregory Linden was an officer in the King's Shropshire Light Infantry. He achieved the rank of Major, but he wasn't out of the "top drawer". His father had been a country parson with no aspirations for elevation to the lofty heights of a bishopric. Then, in 1901, at the age of 39, Grandpa Gregory was killed fighting the Boers in South Africa. Being posthumously mentioned in dispatches didn't pay the bills, but fortunately, Granny Linden had her own money and lived in a world time had put to one side and forgotten about.

In Granny's substantial manor house, built on land owned by her family, you left the modern world outside the front door. You also remembered to take plenty of warm clothing, even in summertime, as there was no central heating or any electric fires to heat the high-ceilinged rooms. Fires blazed downstairs, and in winter, maids would trundle upstairs with buckets of coal for the bedroom grates. But however hard they laboured, I always knew there would be icicles hanging off my windowsill on chilly December mornings.

I was ten years old when I first met Amelia. I remember it vividly. December 24th 1930. The grown-ups were downstairs. Mum, Dad, Granny … that was it. Granny's family had dropped her when she married Grandpa, and while they ensured she had a roof over her head and food on the table, they felt that was where their obligations began and ended. Mum was an only child and so was I. Dad had been adopted when he was a baby and hadn't a clue who his real family were. Was I lonely? What do you think?

I had schoolfriends of course, but Christmas was a time for families, and I simply didn't have siblings and cousins to share the festive joy with. My parents had led similar solitary childhoods, and I was expected to make my own entertainment. Most of the time, I was happy to. I would read, play school with my dolls, and write little plays for them to perform in. Most of the time, I was perfectly content—up to a point. But not that night. For some inexplicable reason, a wave of such despair and loneliness enveloped me that I burst into tears and flung myself on my bed, sobbing into the quilt.

'Do you want to see something amazing?'

I stopped mid sob. The voice was that of a girl. Maybe someone my own age, but there was no one of that description in this house. The youngest maid was probably around fourteen, and this voice belonged to someone younger. I sat up. Through a mist of tears, I could make out a human shape. I wiped my eyes with my hands, and the vision cleared. Standing a few feet away, dressed in Victorian style, a pretty girl smiled at me. Her long blonde hair hung in ringlets, framing a heart-shaped face with the bluest eyes I had ever seen. She looked familiar, although I was certain I had never before met her. She wore a pale blue smock over a white dress trimmed with lace, and her hands were neatly clasped. There was only one thing wrong.

I could see straight through her.

My heart gave a painful thud. 'Who are you?' I asked, my voice barely a whisper. 'Are you a ghost?'

She laughed, showing even white teeth. 'Don't be silly. Of course not. I'm as real as you are. I'm just not here at the same time as you. To me, you seem a bit ghostly. I can see the wall through you.'

'And I can see the wardrobe through you.'

'There you are, then. We're both real and we're both here—just not at the same time. I'm Amelia, by the way.'

'I'm Jo—'

'Josephine. I know. Now, while we *are* here, there's something I want to show you. Come on.' She held out her hand.

I reached for it, but my hand went straight through.

The girl laughed again. 'Silly me. I forgot. Never mind. Follow me. I'll take you.'

She skipped ahead, and I followed, hanging back a little, half of me wondering if I should simply stay put. After all, whether she was a ghost or not, we both knew she wasn't the same as me.

My door was partially open but not wide enough for me to pass through. She managed it by ignoring it completely and slipping through the wall into the corridor outside. I opened the door wider and followed her up a narrow flight of stairs that led to the servants' rooms. My breath caught in my throat. I wasn't supposed to be up here.

Amelia turned. 'Come on, don't dawdle or we'll be too late.'

221

Too late for what? I wondered. I didn't have long to wait, as she stopped outside a closed door.

'You'll have to open that, seeing as we're in your time.'

She sailed through the wall again, while I turned the door handle and pushed.

Inside, a party was in full swing. A small band played. Ladies and gentlemen dressed in all their late Victorian finery waltzed, laughed, and chatted happily. I marvelled at how the women managed to breathe in such tightly corseted dresses designed to show off tiny waists and extravagant bustles. Chandeliers glinted; the polished wood floor shone. In one corner, a fully decorated Christmas tree, complete with candles, twinkled and sparkled. This was no upstairs maids' room. Somehow, the anomaly that allowed Amelia and I to coexist had also transported us to a sumptuous ground floor ballroom in this very house because, despite the altered décor, I recognised the room as the one my parents and granny were currently sitting in, huddled around the fire, playing three-handed whist or some such card game.

I was so taken aback I failed to notice that a young man had come up beside me.

'They can't see you, you know.'

I jumped, and the young man laughed. He moved so that he stood directly in front of me. He was probably in his late teens, undeniably handsome, and smoking a Cuban cigar that gave off a rich, earthy aroma. When he smiled, his eyes crinkled in an endearing way so that even though I was a mere ten years old, my heart fluttered and my cheeks burned.

'I'm Alistair, Amelia's—'

'Ne'er do well brother,' Amelia said.

I reluctantly broke off my fixation with her brother's looks and addressed her. 'Alistair said these people can't see me. Is that true?'

Amelia sighed. 'We're in our time now—mine and Alistair's— so, yes, I'm afraid so, but that doesn't mean you can't enjoy yourself here. You've got me to play with.'

'And me,' Alistair added, blowing out a cloud of smoke.

'You're too old to play girlish games,' Amelia said.

'I won't always be.' An odd comment but I let it pass.

Amelia beckoned me to follow her, and I did so. When I looked over my shoulder to see if he was still there, I could see no sign of Alistair.

Amelia stopped at a buffet table laden with every kind of delicious food. Game pie, pork pie with cranberries, a whole poached salmon, a magnificent baked ham, quails … There were tarts and pies both sweet and savoury. The table practically groaned under the weight. Evidently, the guests would be eating later, as it seemed nothing had yet been touched. Until Amelia started digging in. She must have registered my horrified look.

'Oh, it's all right, no one will notice, and they certainly won't see *you* take any.'

I couldn't argue with that and tried to pick up a piece of pork pie, but of course, this was her world in her time, and I couldn't touch anything, even though I could smell the deliciousness all around me that was making my tummy rumble.

Amelia gave her tinkling laugh again. 'Oh dear, I forgot you couldn't. Never mind.' She popped the remains of a sausage into her mouth and licked her fingers. 'Mama would shoot me if she saw me doing that,' she said, a mischievous glint in her eye. 'Come on, I'd better take you back. Time is getting short.'

I soon learned that time was always short with Amelia. It sped up somehow in her world. An hour with her passed in barely a few minutes of my reality—something I always discovered when I returned. I suppose that's how I was able to feel so close to her on such a short acquaintance.

I trotted after her while continuing to look around for any sign of Alistair. A number of the men were smoking cigars, so I couldn't detect the distinctive aroma of his among so many. Within seconds, we were the other side of the wall, back in my world at my time. I realised for the first time that for the entire stay on the other side, Amelia had lost her transparency. Now we were back, I could see the silent corridor stretching out through her. There was no sound from the other side of the door. I couldn't resist the urge to turn the handle. Locked.

As we made our way slowly back to my room, I asked her the question that was burning in my mind. 'Amelia, how is any of this possible?'

She shrugged her shoulders. 'I don't know. I only know that it *is*. Oh, and I must warn you to be careful of Alistair. He may seem pleasant and affable, but there's something else there. Something ... I'm not sure.' She stopped and so did I. For a second or two, she seemed to fade in and out.

'*Amelia!* What's happening?' And she was back, a smile once again lighting up her face. I breathed a sigh of relief. 'I was worried for a moment. It's so nice to have a friend here. Someone I can talk to.'

'And someone you can share a secret with. You can't tell anyone about what happened tonight. Not about our meeting, the party, anything.'

'And not about Alistair?'

The smile vanished. 'Especially not about Alistair.'

We had reached my door. It was as I had left it. I went to go through, but Amelia held back. 'Aren't you coming in?' I asked.

She shook her head, setting her ringlets bouncing. 'Not now. My time's up here until next Christmas. But I'll see you then, won't I?'

I felt tears pricking my eyelids. To have found a friend here only to have her snatched away was too cruel. 'But a year's such a long time. I'll be coming back in the Spring. For Easter.'

'But I can only come at Christmas. The time will fly. You'll see. Now go back in. Your mother's coming up to say goodnight. I can hear her on the stairs. Can't you? Close your eyes. You'll concentrate better.'

I closed my eyes, listened, but could hear nothing. When I opened them to tell Amelia, she wasn't there. I looked up and down, but there was no sign. Then as I went back into my room, I felt certain I caught the faintest whiff of cigar smoke.

But no one smoked in that house.

~~~~

Christmas Eve 1931 saw me back at Granny's house, in my room after dinner. My heart was racing. Would Amelia come back tonight? She had promised, but did ghosts or spirits or whatever she was keep their promises? I was a year older, but would she have aged? And what about Alistair? The mere thought of his name sent a warm rush through my eleven-year-old body. Night after night, I had clutched my pillow, imagining Alistair's arms around me, caressing my face, and my mind conjured up an image of his smiling face. I could almost smell his cigar …

I tried to be rational about it, of course. I couldn't be in love with someone who didn't exist in my time or place. But was it any more ridiculous than my schoolfriend Rachel's obsession with Clark Gable? She was hardly likely to meet him and have him sweep her off her feet, was she? No more likely than I was to marry Alistair. *Marry?* I really did have it bad.

'You came back, then?'

How could I have missed her entering the room? But suddenly, there she was. My smile couldn't have been any broader as I dived off the bed and rushed forward to greet her, only remembering in time that I couldn't give her the hug I so longed to deliver. Amelia laughed. She looked a little different. Older.

'Your hair,' I said. 'You haven't got ringlets anymore.'

Amelia touched her silky locks, now secured in a demure ponytail that added four years to her looks. 'Ringlets are for babies,' she said, wrinkling her nose. 'I'm a *woman* now. Are you?'

'I'm not sure. I …'

Amelia raised her eyes heavenward. 'Your monthlies. Have they started yet? Mine have. It's been two months now.'

I shook my head and lowered my eyes to try and stem off the embarrassed blush. I failed. Amelia laughed again. 'Yours will start soon enough. Then you'll be a woman too.'

Some of my schoolfriends had already started theirs, and it was like joining an exclusive club. They even behaved differently, as if they were party to a secret the rest of us could only wonder at.

But this was Christmas Eve. My one day with Amelia. Talk of periods and such like would have to wait. I had questions. 'It's so good to see you again, Amelia. What have you been doing? Where have you been? What's it like where you are? How's Alistair—'

This earned me another laugh from my ethereal friend. 'So many questions. We need to get to the party. Alistair's there, so you can ask him yourself. Come with me now and I'll try and answer you on the way, but hurry. There's not a lot of time.'

Out in the corridor, we walked, and Amelia talked. 'I've been at home mostly, studying with my new governess.' She pulled a face. 'A real martinet. Miss Gibson, she's called. I intend her stay shall be short. The other day, she pulled my hair so hard she ended up with a clump of it in her hand. Mama refused to believe me because when she's around, Miss Gibson is the soul of propriety, but I honestly think she hates girls. Probably children in general. Of course, Alistair's at university, so he doesn't have to put up with her. Anyway, he went to Harrow. It's only because I'm a girl that I'm not allowed to go to school. Mama is too afraid I'll become a bluestocking and end up on the shelf with no hope of securing a good husband because I'll frighten them away with my book learning!' She giggled. 'Is it better in your time, Josephine? Do girls like us go to school?'

'Well, I do. Lots of upper-class girls don't, though. They still have governesses.'

'They're bred to breed, like me.' Amelia sighed. 'Such a waste. Never mind, at least *you* get to go. What's it like?'

I shrugged. I wasn't a particular fan of school, although I did enjoy English and History, and my friends, of course. 'It's all right. Some of the teachers are very nice. We have one who's horrible. Like your Miss Gibson. But tell me more about your life. Where do you live? Why do you come here only on Christmas Eve?'

'I live … well, here …' She spread her arms expansively. 'This is my home too. Oh, look, no more time for questions. We're here now.'

'But …'

'No, we must go in now or it will be too late.'

'What would happen if it was too late?'

Amelia shook her head and disappeared through the wall.

As I had the previous year, I turned the handle, and the door opened easily. Inside, the party was in full swing, the table laden, dancers in high spirits. And Alistair …

'That's a pretty dress.'

I spun around, almost falling into his arms, except, of course, I couldn't and would have fallen flat on my face if I hadn't righted myself in time.

'Th—thank you,' I stuttered, feeling stupid and childish.

Alistair smiled. He, too, looked different. A pencil moustache adorned his upper lip. It suited him and gave him a more mature air. 'You're such a tonic, Josephine. So different to all these silly empty-headed girls.' He gave a dismissive gesture with his hand as if consigning all the females in the room to some invisible waste bin. 'I have a mind to wait until you grow up and then ask for your hand in marriage. Do you think your father would approve of me?'

I stared at him in disbelief. Was this a proposal? Was I dreaming?

Amelia drifted back from wherever she had gone. I hadn't even noticed her leave. 'Alistair, what *are* you doing now? Poor Josephine looks like she's just seen a ghost. Oh!' Her laughter rang out, drawing attention from some of the nearest couples. 'But that's exactly what she thinks *we* are.'

'Whereas we know we're real and *she* is the one who has passed over.'

'Alistair!' Amelia's shocked expression took my breath away. 'That was uncalled for. You know the rules, and now you've broken them. Come, Josephine, we have to go.'

'But it isn't time,' Alistair protested.

Around us, the room was growing darker. Amelia seemed agitated. She kept glancing quickly around her as if scared of something.

'What is it, Amelia? What are you frightened of?'

'Alistair should have known better. Stupid fool. He's ruined it.'

But Alistair wasn't around to hear her admonishment. No one was. We were out in the corridor again, with the door shut and no sound of any party wafting through.

Amelia had tears in her eyes. 'I can't come back with you tonight, Josephine. I'm so sorry.'

My heart went out to my special friend, along with a burning desire to get back to Alistair … my betrothed. 'Will I see you next year? On Christmas Eve?'

'I think so. I hope so. Be there in your room, and I will try and come to you. Don't forget, though. Say nothing to anyone about our visits.'

'I promise.'

'Now close your eyes. You cannot see me leave.'

'Why?'

'It's against the rules, and too many have already been broken tonight.'

I closed my eyes. 'Happy Christmas, Amelia.'

No reply. After a few seconds, I opened them. The corridor was empty.

~~~~

1931 gave way to 1932. I counted the months, weeks, days, and hours until I could see Amelia and Alistair again. At last, it was Christmas and our arrival at Granny's.

She seemed more stooped and appeared to have aged five years since Easter when we had last seen her. Mum was worried. She and Dad had spoken in hushed whispers about her various ailments. Arthritis, a stomach ulcer, trouble with her breathing, terrible headaches, and difficulty keeping food down. She had lost a lot of weight, and her hands were like a little bird's claws. Her eyes, too, had lost too much of their shine. A dull grey had replaced the bright blue. Her mind also seemed out of kilter somehow. She could be perfectly lucid one minute, and the next, she rambled off in a world of her own. Not a happy one either, judging by her sad expression. Mum told me to play along with her. If Granny Linden said something that didn't quite make sense, I was to nod politely or say yes.

On Christmas Eve afternoon, Mum and Dad went out for a long walk down the country lanes. I had been instructed to sit with Granny and keep her company.

The fire blazed in the hearth, and Granny sat, her favourite shawl around her shoulders, staring into the flames, saying nothing while I read a book.

The logs crackled and sent out a shower of sparks. Fortunately, the fireguard caught them all, but the sudden noise acted as some sort of trigger on Granny.

'Milly's been a very silly girl,' she said.

'Has she?' I asked, wondering who Milly was. 'What has she done?'

'Been with that boy. I told her he was up to no good, but she would have him. Now I don't know what Mama is going to say, and as for Papa ...'

'Which boy is that?' I asked.

Granny looked up and straight into my eyes. 'What boy?'

'The one you just mentioned. The one Milly's been with?'

'How do you know about that?'

'You just said Milly had been a silly girl and she'd been with some boy or other.'

'You're not supposed to know about that. No one is supposed to know about that.' Granny returned her gaze to the fire, her lips moving but no sound emerging.

I set my book aside, unable to concentrate.

~~~~

At the sound of Mum and Dad opening the front door, I raced out into the hall to greet them. I told them what Granny had said. 'Do you know anyone called Milly?'

Mum thought for a moment. 'Only Amelia. She may have been called Milly. I don't know. I never knew her. She died in childbirth. Terrific scandal, I believe. She wasn't married, you see.' Mum clapped her hands to either side of her face. 'Oh God, yes, now I remember.'

'What?' Dad asked. I couldn't speak. I was still reeling from the mention of the name *Amelia*.

Mum lowered her hands. 'Come on, let's go into the kitchen. I've got to get this straight in my head. It's been years since I heard about it, and that was from one of the maids, so how reliable the story is, I'm not at all sure. Although she *was* here in service at the time.'

We sat at the scrubbed pine table. Fortunately, Cook was having her afternoon nap, so we were alone. Mum laid her hands flat on the surface. 'According to Lily, Mama had a sister called Amelia who was a couple of years younger than her. She was always a bit wayward and liked to make sure she got her own way. Her mother was a little stricter, but she could twist her father around her

232

little finger, so when she took against a governess once, the woman was summarily dismissed and left within twenty-four hours, without a reference.'

'Miss Gibson,' I whispered.

'Who?' Mum asked. She shook her head dismissively. 'I don't know her name. Anyway, when Amelia was about seventeen, she fell headlong in love with a quite unsuitable young man from the village. I don't know his name or anything about him other than it appears he got her pregnant and that was the last anyone saw of him. Well, I say anyone … One person saw him again. His murderer.'

'Someone killed Amelia's boyfriend?' This Christmas Eve night was going to be interesting.

Mum nodded. 'Apparently. And the smart money was on one candidate. Amelia and Honoria's older brother. Alistair.'

I nearly fell off my chair.

'Are you all right, Jo?' Dad asked. 'You look as pale as a ghost.'

I winced at the comparison. 'I'm fine, Dad. It's just so much to take in.'

Mum sighed. 'Oh well, you're old enough, you might as well know the rest of it. I'll guarantee there's not a soul for miles around who wouldn't happily regale you with the same tale. Alistair was a thoroughly bad lot. He was sent down from Oxford in his second year for gambling debts, among other things, and it was rumoured that he had an unhealthy obsession with young women. The younger, the better, not to put too fine a point on it. He also had carnal feelings towards his sister Amelia. She apparently did not return those feelings, but she was of an age when hormones play a large part, and while she may have resisted any advances her brother made, she certainly made eyes at any other young man who took her fancy.' Mum stopped. 'I need a drink.'

Dad stood and went to fetch a glass from a cupboard. Once he had filled it with cold water, he set it down in front of her, and she drank half of it in one go.

I cleared my throat. 'What happened to Alistair?'

Mum set her glass down. 'All I know is that one night, he disappeared and has never been seen or heard from since. Amelia's baby was stillborn, and she died of fever three days later. Now you must promise never to speak of any of this to Granny. It will upset her far too much. Is that understood?'

I nodded. 'I wouldn't have mentioned it at all if she hadn't said what she did.'

'I know. I can't think why after all these years. I have never heard her mention Amelia's name, or Alistair's, come to that. Maybe they talk about them up at the big house, but Mama?' She shook her head. 'Never.'

'Is Lily still alive?' I asked.

'Oh gracious no. She was an old woman when she told me the story. She said she thought I had a right to know. She died before you were born. Now I think we should get back to Granny.' Mum stood, and Dad followed suit.

I pushed my chair back. What would I say to Amelia tonight? Or Alistair, come to that. In the personae I encountered them, did they even know what fate awaited them? Did Alistair run away, or was there some sort of foul play involved? I would have to handle this carefully if I was ever to discover the truth.

~~~~

'I thought I would surprise you.'

The familiar voice came from behind me. I jumped off the bed. Amelia smiled at me. She was dressed in a lilac gown with décolleté more suited to a young woman than a girl of thirteen. Her hair was piled on her head in a style that owed a great deal to the skill and artistry of a trained stylist or, most probably, lady's maid. White kid gloves encased her hands and covered her slim arms up to her elbows. Diamonds glittered in her ears and around her neck.

'Oh, Amelia, you look beautiful. But so much older. Are you really the same age as me?'

She laughed. 'Not any longer, Josephine. I've leapt ahead a little. I'm sixteen now. But come on, the party won't wait for us.'

'After last year, I wondered if you would be able to come back.'

Amelia avoided my eyes. 'It wasn't easy. But I wanted to so much … So here I am. Come on.'

This year, as before, everyone was having a great time. I accompanied her, but as always, they couldn't see me. I did see some averted eyes from a number of the ladies as Amelia passed them, and one older woman snapped her fan shut with an angry tutting, her face like a thunderstorm. The men, on the other hand, clearly appreciated a pretty face. There was some ribald laughter which I didn't like. It held an unpleasant edge to it.

Alistair surprised me once again. 'Utterly charming, Josephine. That dress brings out the blue in your eyes.'

Remembering last year, I took a breath before turning to greet him. Still enamoured, I couldn't speak at first and felt awkward and tongue-tied. Then an unwelcome thought struck me. I was actually related to this man. He was Granny's brother, so that made him my Great Uncle Alistair. A wave of nausea swept up from the pit of my stomach. I couldn't be in love with my own great uncle. It was obscene.

He smiled. The moustache was gone, and his cleanshaven face suited him far better. As with Amelia, he was around four years older than when I had last seen him.

'Let me see now,' he said. 'You must be thirteen. Am I right?'

I nodded, still unable to speak.

'Old enough, then.'

Old enough for what? I wanted to ask but daren't. I had a feeling the answer might not be one I wanted to hear.

Alistair closed his eyes for a moment. 'I'm picturing you. If I could just take you in my arms and—'

'*No!*' I yelled as loudly as I ever had in my life. 'Get away from me. That's disgusting. I'm your niece. My mother is your sister's daughter.'

'Josephine, whatever's the matter?' Amelia was at my side. 'What have you done, Alistair. What did you say to her?'

He smiled, but it was more like a sneer. 'Nothing you haven't heard before, dear sister.'

'You fool. You've ruined everything now. *Everything.*'

They were attracting an audience while the band played on. I heard random snippets of conversation from men and women alike, some accompanied by laughter:

'I hear Alistair likes to keep it in the family,'

'She's nothing but a common trollop.'

'The baker's boy was boasting about bedding her.'

'I heard she's got herself in the family way.'

All through this, Alistair and Amelia stared at each other, until the last comment, which her brother couldn't fail to have heard.

'Is that true?' he asked.

'Is what true?'

'That you're …' He glanced down below her waistline.

Amelia drew herself up and cast a defiant look around the assembled riveted throng. In a clear voice, she announced, 'Yes,' to the accompaniment of shocked gasps. A couple of women had to be steadied, and the pungent aroma of smelling salts assailed my nose.

The room darkened. The sound of the band faded, and as I stood in disbelief, the scene played out in front of me like a theatre set being invisibly struck. Within seconds, everything in the room had simply melted away, leaving nothing but an empty servants' room in the attic of my grandmother's house. I stood frozen to the spot, willing everything to go back to how it had been before … on that first Christmas when Amelia and I first met. Before innocence was lost forever and darkness replaced the light. But I had to accept that the fantasy was over, so, reluctantly, I turned and left that haunted place.

I crept downstairs, too scared and sad to be alone. In the warm drawing room, I found my parents and Granny Linden. She had been crying, her eyes reddened and brimming with tears. Mum was kneeling in front of her, clasping her hands. All eyes turned to me as I entered.

'Come and sit with us,' Mum said, her voice quiet and calm. 'Granny wants to tell you something.'

I pulled up a stool close to Granny and next to Mum. The fire crackled and warmed me. I hadn't realised how cold it had been upstairs in that attic.

'I know, Jo,' Granny said. 'I know what's been happening these past few years. Every Christmas Eve from when you were ten. I know because she told me. Milly. Amelia to you. She comes to me a lot these days. One day, she'll come and take me, and that will be that. It won't be long now. I was with her, you see, all through those three days of labour. She suffered. Oh, how that poor girl suffered. She wouldn't give up, though. She wanted to have that baby, especially after what happened to the father. She loved him, you see. Tommy Ryder, the baker's son. I didn't care for him. Cocky. Boastful. He thought fathering a child with Amelia would be his passport into the aristocracy, but Alistair wasn't having that. On the night of the annual Christmas party, he took a shotgun and killed Tommy. Then he buried him deep in the woods out there. Amelia was heavily pregnant at the time.'

I stared at her in disbelief. 'But I was there. At that party. She told everyone she was having a baby, but there was no sign yet.'

Granny sighed. 'Illusions. A whole chimera of them. Milly showed you what she wanted you to see. In reality, when Alistair told her what he'd done, the shock brought on premature labour. He told her they could go away together, live as man and wife where no one knew them, and no one would know, although what they would live on was another matter. Amelia flew into a rage. She attacked Alistair—told him she never wanted to see him again. So, he left. The gamekeeper found his body in the potting shed. He had shot himself through the head. Of course, it was all hushed up, but Amelia knew because the gamekeeper told her. And as she lay dying, she told me.' Granny bowed her head. Tears streamed down her cheeks.

'It's all right, Mama,' Mum said, stroking her forehead. 'It's all such a long time ago.'

Granny gasped, and her sobs stopped. 'But it isn't, Irene. That's the whole point. That's why Jo has been having these experiences. When Milly was expecting, she somehow knew she was having a girl. She had a name ready for her. She called her Josephine. On the night Jo was born, Milly came to see me. She told me. Jo is *her* daughter. Amelia died on Christmas Eve, vowing to watch over her little girl even though she knew the child had been stillborn.'

Mum dropped Granny's hands. 'My God. I saw her too. I thought I was dreaming, but I saw her. The first night. You were so sick, Jo. We thought we were going to lose you and we didn't even have a name for you yet. Then I saw … Milly … it must have been. She bent over your cot and whispered, "Josephine," and in an instant, you started to rally. I thought I'd imagined seeing the … apparition … but it really happened.'

Granny nodded. 'I'm afraid it did.'

'Afraid?' I asked.

Granny's sigh seemed to emanate from the depths of her soul, and it appeared to echo around the room even though I knew that wasn't possible. 'Milly shouldn't have done what she did. Like her child, you weren't meant to survive more than a few hours after birth. You were an innocent until my sister bent over you that first night. Milly passed the soul of her dead baby into your body through her breath. She played with fate, and there's always a price to pay. You must understand, my sister was lost to the good the night she first lay with her brother. She was eleven years old, and it was on Christmas Eve when Alistair took her as a husband takes a wife. She was never the same after that. It ... unhinged something in her brain. And now, all these years later, she's back to claim what she believes is hers. You, Jo, but the price for what she did the night you were born remains unpaid, and that cannot be allowed.'

The echoing grew louder. Granny's lips moved, but her words seemed to bounce back and forth off the walls in random waves, leaving me reeling, turning this way and that, trying to follow the sound. The room grew darker, and the figures of my mother and grandmother were fading, becoming less distinct and tangible. I cried out to them, but my words were swallowed up in the creeping mist seeping from the walls, enveloping everything it touched. Out of it, one lone figure emerged.

'Amelia,' I whispered, but the room magnified the sound of my words until it became a deafening roar, swirling around me faster and faster while I cowered on the floor and watched Amelia. She was laughing. Enjoying the scene.

Her voice sliced through me. 'Remember, Josephine?'

And I remembered. Only *this* time, it was happening all around me. In *my* time, not hers. I stared in horror as, once again, the scene I had witnessed upstairs played out. It seemed I watched it all while insulated in some sort of bubble. I tried to move. I screamed, but physically, nothing touched me. The crackling fire was lost in a heap of cold ashes as the drawing room folded in on itself, taking my grandmother and my parents with it.

Then it stopped.

Silence.

I alone was left in a derelict shell of a room. Amelia Swann, or whatever it was of her that had projected itself to me, had also vanished. It was as if none of it had ever happened. Sometimes, even now, I wonder if it ever did.

⁓⁓⁓⁓

That was all so long ago. I have never seen Amelia since that night, although I have come to believe that I never really did meet her. Not the real Amelia—only her chimera, the soul that was damaged all those years ago. And still I wait, for I know it isn't over. Granny had the answer. "There is always a price to pay," she said. And I am charged with paying it.

Time means nothing now; except I am aware of growing older—even though I am in spirit. Somehow, I know it's Christmas Eve. Something has changed in my strange and unreal world. In front of me, a new corridor stretches. Is this the time? With nowhere else to go, I start down it.

<u>Catherine Cavendish</u>

Cat first started writing when someone thrust a pencil into her hand as a child. She writes mainly supernatural, Gothic, ghostly, and haunted house horror, with some folk horror added to the mix. Her books include: *The Stones of Landane, Those Who Dwell in Mordenhyrst Hall, The After-Death of Caroline Rand,* and the Nemesis of the Gods trilogy, among others.

You can find her at <u>catherinecavendish.com</u> and other social media.